Can't Buy Me Love

(1964-1967)

A novel

Volume One
THE COST OF LOVING
SERIES

Martin Humphries

Table of Contents

To enjoy your ***FREE*** copy of the fun-filled novella '***Fun Is On Its Way***', a prequel to '***The Cost of Loving***' series, and to join the growing list of Sophia's followers, be sure to follow this link below.

http://www.martinhumphriesauthor.com/free-novella

Oscar Wilde once famously said…

"Everything in the world is about sex except sex. Sex is about power."

But that's not quite true, is it? Because

"Everything in the world is about sex and money except sex and money. Sex is about power. Money is about power and freedom."

Join our heroine as she discovers how to use both to her advantage…

Prologue

I remembered the feel of him - of it - as I leaned forward and offered Celia the photograph. It was a perfectly ordinary photograph, except that it almost always made me cry. It was black and white and showed my brother, my father, my mother and me all kneeling in the sand. My brother was misbehaving - as usual - and refused to look at the camera simply because my mother had wanted the photograph taken.

Something to remember the holiday by, she had said.

Hmm. Some memory. Some holiday.

I was kneeling in front of my father.

His arm was across my torso.

His body held tightly against me.

The memories all came flooding back as I looked at that photograph again. The stiffness of that part of my father that I was too young to really understand - and his obsession with it - pressed into my back.

The anxious look in my eyes.

The hungry look in his.

How old was I then? Thirteen I think.

Not long before my life changed.

Forever.

Doesn't look anything like me now, does it? I asked Celia, with a wry smile.

Celia shook her head.

I can't believe how much I've changed from that roly-poly, mop-haired wallflower of a girl that you see there.

We all laughed, but mine was more one of irony as I stared again at the photograph. I thought how happy we all looked. How happy my father looked - the bastard who got the better of me before I got the better of him - and how photographs lie.

I slipped the photograph back into my bag.

Yes, I said. In fact, I'll tell you the whole story. From A to Z. We have all evening.

It really all started in the mid-sixties, not long after that photograph was taken. What a time that was for a young girl like me. I became a true reflection of those times, much to my amazement, because my stars did not look well aligned and my trajectory looked miserably short.

But I was wrong.

Change really was everywhere - on the wind, in the air - change, change, everywhere. Even my name got changed. And yet, so often, we just took it all for granted. Wasn't this just normal progress? I look back now and am amazed by the depth and ferocity of it. The joy, the anger, the excitement, the sorrow and then victory - almost always victory.

Of course, you're too young to remember much of it, Celia, except what you've read in the history books and seen on TV, but there's been nothing like it since that would give you any idea of how exhilarating it all was.

It was a time when change meant death in the streets, blood in the gutters, gunshots and mayhem - a time of crashing, ding-dong, smack-across-the-head changes. We're talking about women's liberation, equal pay, free love, student protests, black power and civil rights, Stonewall, smoking pot, call girls, call boys, gay rights, Mary Quant, mini-skirts, kinky boots, Carnaby Street, King's Road, pop music, rock music, The Beatles, The Rolling Stones, Cilla Black – yes, Cilla Black, queen of Saturday night TV - long hair, Helen Gurley Brown, the pill!

I mean - seriously - this was a revolution.

People were discovering a whole new way to live, and never before had women been able to follow their dreams without the usual constraints of family and society.

Really, you have no idea.

Yes, it really was an amazing decade to be young and female and huge fun for a girl like me. I was born Edith Butt - what a name - shortly after the war on a council estate in Croydon. My mother was good-hearted but useless and empty-headed. My father enjoyed a few too many pints and physical violence as the answer to almost every problem. What a bastard he was, I said, as the memories bombarded me like angry hornets disturbed from their hidden nest.

But I owe my transformation from fat, plain and abused teenager, complete with an over-sized inferiority complex, to my wonderful cousin, Ronnie, and three of the most remarkable people of that extraordinary decade. Helen Gurley Brown, who liberated women's minds, Mary Quant, who liberated women's bodies and Carl Djerassi, who liberated women's sexuality.

Celia looked quizzical.

You don't know Carl Djerassi? You should google him. You, and people like you, have a lot to thank him for. How old are you? Thirty-eight, isn't it? That means you were born in 1987, right?

I laughed.

My big excitement was all over before you were even born. For me, the magic started one Saturday night in March 1964 when my father returned home from the pub. He decided to give my mother a black right eye, to go with the already black left one, plus a few bruises for good measure, while my darling brother looked on with words of encouragement. Such was my sad and wretched home life and, although not a lot worse than other pathetic families in that miserable place, it was mine and I hated it.

My mother seemed to adore my father and naturally assumed she was entirely to blame and deserved it all. She took it in good spirit, and with few tears, except of regret for the things she had convinced herself that she must surely have done to deserve it.

But then, Celia, on that Saturday night, it all completely and utterly changed.

I picked up my glass of wine, took a long, cool gulp and let the story unfold.

1

To the Rescue

Ronnie's story...

"Do you think he's diddling her?" Mum asked one Sunday as we all sat quietly eating our roast dinner.

I liked to come home for those as often as I could because - well, let's face it - I was a young man living on my own and, of course, I couldn't cook for toffee and certainly not like my mother could. Normally, the conversation was idle at best, but not today.

Something was niggling at her.

"Well, that makes a change from 'pass the gravy', I suppose. You've got my attention." That was my father. He, normally, just liked to eat and not get involved in issues that might divert him from concentrating on his food, especially Sunday lunch.

We both stared at her.

"Well, it's just that I was talking to Evey yesterday and she was quite angry about Billy. She never gets angry about Billy. She's a total softy where that husband of hers is concerned, but she's worried about Edith, I can tell. For somebody who keeps her blinkers firmly in place that only means more trouble as far as I'm concerned."

"Yes, but that doesn't mean that he's being a naughty boy with his own daughter. Honestly, I don't know where you get these ideas from sometimes, Stella, I really don't." Dad was rolling his eyes.

"From my brain, Freddie. From my brain. Where I do my thinking, which is what you should be doing sometimes. This is family we're talking about. My family. My sister." Mum wagged her fork at dad's face and poked her tongue out at him. "You should show more concern. Anyway, I'd bet you the crown jewels that that's behind all this."

"What?"

"That he's diddling his own daughter! You know as well as I do that he's made his mind up she's not his. Are you going to change that for him? Good luck!"

"You don't believe that, do you?" I chimed in.

"It doesn't matter two figs what I believe, Ronnie. It's all about what your uncle Billy thinks and if that's what he thinks then nobody's going to change his mind for him. Only he can do that. But, knowing him, I bet he's taking it out on Evey - and Edith, poor thing - just to get his own back."

"I hate to say this but she's no catch, Mum. Why would anybody have a go at her?"

She rolled her eyes. "It's got nothing to do with her looks. It's all about vengeance. He's getting his own back the only way that bastard knows how to."

"Stella, language at the dinner table."

That was my dad again.

Silly arse.

"Dad, we're all grown up here, don't forget. I think we can have the odd bastard over the dinner table and an occasional bugger and shit."

"Ronnie that's enough."

My mother this time.

Silly cow.

"I swore because I'm upset. You know how I am when we talk about that pig and my sister and the miserable life he's created for her. For them. And besides, Edith wasn't always like that and that's what makes me wonder."

"Wonder what?"

"What he's done to her, silly! To turn her from a kid who was full of life to that drab and lifeless rag of a girl she is today."

And that, I had to admit, was true.

Being a decade older than Edith, I had seen her grow from a baby to a child to a girl and now to a wretch. It was sad to see the light in her eyes go out and to watch as she became a moody, sulky, miserable girl with a temper that sometimes she could barely control. Mum was probably right. Edith's anger and aggression were, no doubt, a defense against her vulnerability and feelings of helplessness.

And it was sad to see.

She had been a fun-loving, lively kid and her world was all about the three W's – where, when, why? Question after question after question until you thought she couldn't know more if she'd swallowed every volume of the Encyclopedia Britannica. She wanted to know the reason for everything.

And then she didn't.

That had all been well and truly kicked out of her now. She had become an empty vessel which we all wanted to fill up again. As a child she had shone and sometimes dazzled, but that light had flickered and died - that glow of a child revelling in the exploration of life.

I, for one, wanted to re-ignite it.

Why me?

Because I had been there myself.

Being queer in the fifties and sixties, you don't survive without having the shit kicked out of you.

Sometimes for real.

I was one of the lucky ones.

I almost drowned, surfaced, found something to hold on to and survived, but you always stay water-logged no matter how hard you try to dry out. My light had extinguished and been reignited, but only a flicker remained.

The intensity was gone.

Just like Edith's.

Maybe it will come back.

Maybe, in time, I'll forget the mornings when I would wake up disappointed that I hadn't drowned. Forget the helplessness, the hopelessness and the days when life didn't seem the favoured option.

All that fear and confusion.

It all seems like self-pity, I know, but I only have one thing to say about that – what the fuck do you know? Just you try it.

And so I knew that, whatever Edith was struggling with, it was ugly and wretched and, quite possibly, life-threatening. That bright, lively, bubbly, inquisitive child who used to bob and sway like a balloon searching for more height with which to explore all of the world, stretching out far, far ahead.

What's this?

What's that?

Where's the other?

Question after question after question, only to burst and sink, deflated, to a weedy, miserable corner of the earth where she could hide, abandoned, in a dreary place with no way that she knew of to free herself.

I saw myself reflected in those sad, deep pools whenever I looked into her eyes, and I wanted her to know that there *was* a way out and I would help her limp through it and get strong again. All she needed was someone standing in her corner. Someone strong enough to fight for her in the same way that I had longed, when I was her age, to have someone there to fight for me, as I struggled with my own demons.

"So what are we going to do about it?" I said.

"What can we do? I'm her auntie but that doesn't give me any rights."

"Can't we report him to the police?"

"For what? Beating his wife? They don't care about stuff like that."

"You don't want to go dragging the police into it. It's just family stuff."

Dad again.

Daft sod.

"So, it's alright to go bashing your missus about, is it? 'Cos you only have to try that once with me, matey, and I'll have your bollocks off and in the bird feeder."

"Calm down, will you? All I meant was that if you call in the police for your sister then you'd have to call them in to half the families on that estate. It's just normal family stuff. Wives get a bashing. It happens. It's no big deal."

"No big deal? I'll take a swing for you one day and see how you like it." Mum was almost shouting now. "And I know it happens alright. But kids don't get messed about with where they shouldn't ought. Then it's time for the police."

"Oh, yeah? And where's the proof? Your sister wouldn't say a word against that teddy-boy husband of hers; he can do no wrong in her eyes."

"I bet she would, you know. If push came to shove. She won't hear a word said against him but it's not love that does that. It's fear. She's afraid of him. She's afraid of him leaving her. She's bloody afraid of everything is that one."

Mum stabbed another roast potato, dripping with gravy, and raised it to her lips. She looked at both of us in turn with a fierce look that had a decision emblazoned across it.

"Mum, that was delicious. Now what's for 'dee-ssert'?" I said, stretching the word with my best American drawl.

Mum smiled the smile of a happy cook before her contented and admiring audience. "Glad you liked it. And you've been picking up too many words from that sister of yours. It's still pudding in this house, mate, and don't you forget it. Soon you'll be asking for cookies and toemaytoes."

"So? What's for pudding?"

"Your favourite. Trifle."

I swooned.

Mums.

Sometimes it was worth coming home.

"Mum! I love you."

"Don't be so soft," she said and smiled. "It's only a bleedin' trifle." Then, just as she was about to start clearing up the dishes, she paused. "I think I'll pay her another visit next weekend."

"Who?"

"You know. My stupid sister - Evey."

Ah. So that was the decision behind that fierce look.

2

The Great Escape

Edith's story...

My aunt Stella, my mother's sister, dropped by at just about the time my mother's right eye had changed colour enough to match the left, and my aunt wasn't impressed. I had caught a glancing blow as well, which was now bruising nicely.

"God, Evelyn! Has he been at it again?" Stella cried, as my mother opened the front door. "I bloody well hope he's not in, is he? Because I shan't be responsible for my actions and I might be the one to regret it."

"No, he's gone down the pub."

"Oh, right. That'll make it alright then, won't it? Get pissed and forget it ever happened. For heaven's sake, Evey, you've got to do something about it. You can't go on like this. Report him – or leave him."

"I can't do that. He needs me and, besides, he doesn't mean it. He's a good man really. He's always sorry afterwards."

"Good man, my arse! He's a sodding bastard, is what he is. I never trusted him from the moment I saw him feeling up your bridesmaid at your wedding."

"But all men are like that."

"All men most certainly are not like that, and certainly not on their wedding day. I'd have ripped his balls off if he'd done that to me. You've got to stand up for yourself, Evey. Teach him that he can't get away with stuff like that." Her sigh was deeply disapproving. "And what about Edith? How do you think she's going to come out of all this? Not well, I can tell you that right now."

Stella turned to me, smiled and took my hand. "Tell you what, pet. Pack a bag and come home with me. You can stay as long as you like and get away from all this. I'm sick of seeing you both so miserable all the time. And I won't take any argument from you, Evelyn. God knows you haven't been much help to her so far."

I smiled feebly but, inwardly, I was excited.

More than excited.

This was the moment I had longed for.

Was this my great escape?

Grab it and run.

Maybe I'll never have to see this place, or my father, ever again.

"Can I, Mum?"

"You don't have to ask her. Anyway, Evey, you wouldn't say no, would you? You'd better bloody well not, anyway, or this time I just might report him to the authorities." Stella smiled and squeezed my hand. "You're coming home with me, my girl, and that's an end to it. Go on, pack a bag. The getaway car's outside. Well, getaway bus actually."

It was my getaway bus.

Get away for good bus.

I dashed off to my room and threw as much as I could in a duffel bag, crammed all my Beatles' records into a paper carrier bag, and rushed back to join them.

"Are you sure you won't come too?" Stella asked my mother, putting her face up close and giving Mum a gentle look of sisterly intimacy. "I know you've always said no but you should think again, if only for a short while."

Mum shook her head gently and answered softly. "No. I'll stay here. He needs me you know, despite it all. And I need him. I can't explain it. I just know that's how it has to be."

"That's not how it has to be at all, and you know it! There's just no talking to you. Never is." Stella sighed, exasperated. "Anyway, you know where we live and you only have to call and I'll be over to get you. But, Evey love, try and put your foot down with him. Put up some resistance or he'll just keep walking all over you." She gave her sister a hug. "But, in the meantime, this one comes with me," she cried, pointing her finger violently in my direction. "If I can't save you, I'm bloody well going to try and save her."

Numerous times before she had tried to get my mother to leave and once again she wouldn't, so she took me instead. You can't imagine how much I had longed for that day.

Just a few train stops and a bus ride from Croydon and I would be in another world. It was nothing special - just a piece of uninspired suburban London - but to me it really was another world, bordering on heaven. My aunt had been much like my mother but, whereas my mother had been beaten down, insulted, abused and humiliated, Stella had been worshipped and adored by Freddie, her husband of more than twenty-five years. He had worked hard to provide for her and their two children, Norma and Ronald. Because of that, they lived comfortably on a leafy suburban street with neat and spacious gardens and splendid brick-built homes that exuded safety and security, politeness and civility. I had always dreamed of such a home and now it looked as if I just might get one.

Freddie had what it took to succeed and my father did not. Years ago, his grandfather had arrived in England from Italy, married and stayed. Freddie had worked hard to turn a job on a construction team into a home building company that enjoyed modest success, thanks to being located in suburban London, as it grew and grew and grew after the Second World War.

Stella had thrived on it and she became my idol. She rarely visited our home but my mother and I often visited hers. I was so envious of my cousins who took all this love and affection so much for granted that I wanted to scream at them for not realising how incredibly lucky they were. For Stella, this meant nice clothes, a lovely home and time to look after herself. And I was on my way there now, perhaps to make it my home too, please god!

"You'll be much better off with us, Edith. You mark my words," Stella reached over and patted my hand as we made our way through the grey, drab streets of South London. Sitting silently upstairs on the double-decker bus, I stared at the ever-changing streets, the people walking - some strolling, some rushing, some scowling, some smiling - and wondered what their lives were like.

What they went home to.

"You're well out of it, love," Stella said softly. She could tell I was close to tears but she didn't know they were more tears of joy at the prospect of being released from my former life. "Your dad always was a sod. I never told your mum, but he even made a play for me at her wedding. And me with Freddie sitting right there. He didn't care, your dad." Stella spoke wistfully. "You know, your mum could have had anybody she wanted. She was pretty - still is - happy and full of fun. But she just fell for your dad, hook, line and sinker. And sink her, he did," she sighed.

"Why did she marry him then if she could have done better?"

"Ah! That's the million dollar question, isn't it? Love's got a lot to answer for and, if you're smart, you'll keep well away from it unless you know it's going to be good for you. But then love's clever. It deceives you until it's too late."

"It worked for you and Uncle Freddie, didn't it?"

"Ah, yes, but I didn't love him that much – but don't ever tell him I said so. One day I thought 'he's the right man for me' and that was that … didn't need to go looking for that head over heels stuff. That's far too dangerous. I mean, look what it's done to your mother – ruined her."

We rode on into the darkness and the grimy city streets turned into a whole new world of spacious, tree-lined suburban avenues.

A world where everything looked cleaner, fresher, brighter and well -scrubbed.

The world I wanted.

"You know the trouble with your dad back then was that he was too smooth and good looking for his own good. Thought he could get away with murder. We don't exactly come from royalty, me and your mum, but we were pretty respectable and him an odd-jobbing good-for-nothing, in my opinion." Stella sniffed as if a bad smell had hit her. "He saw your mum as a catch and made it his business to win her. Trouble was, he did. And, once he had, he was stuck with her and, in time, he resented her for it. His ball and chain was on him and no mistake. Then it went from good to bad to worse and now look at the mess you're all in." Stella sighed and put her arm around my shoulders. "No, trust me on this one, sweetheart, forget love and stick to like. It lasts longer and it's a lot better for you." She looked at me and winked. "Take it from me, love. I'm speaking from experience. Oh! Here's our stop. Press the bell."

We got off the bus and made our way to their comfortable suburban home, daydreams of newfound daily joy bubbling and bouncing around inside my head. Stella carried my duffle bag and I clung tightly to my Beatles records, the source of all my pleasure and the only comfort that I had been able to suck out of my recent life.

Stella noticed.

"Hanging on to those records for dear life, aren't you?"

I gave her a wide-eyed sideways glance as we marched briskly homewards.

"They mean the world to me."

"Really? That mop-headed bunch?" She chuckled. "They can barely hold a tune."

"How can you say that?" It was like heresy to me.

"Well. Each one to their own, I suppose."

I used to retreat to my bedroom, slip a Beatles record onto my Dansette player and, with earphones borrowed from my brother, who was rarely home, I would drift away into a different world of joy and ecstasy as the music swirled around my brain like some exotic drug. Theirs was music like no other and, as I closed my eyes, I would be transported to another place and time; I couldn't wait to do it again.

Music had never sounded so good.

Or so different.

Or so strange.

As her and Freddie's house hove into view, I realized that that was what she had strived for most; not love, but comfort, security and a bit of prestige. But, for all her social climbing, she still cared about her sister and because family bonds are strong, no matter what, she also cared about me.

To my credit, I had always been a good girl. I was intelligent, quiet and shy, which meant that I was totally overwhelmed by the ugly side of my home life. In my neighbourhood, to be stupid, lazy, rude and obnoxious earned you some pretty good marks. Where the ability to survive and flourish at the evolutionary level of slime stood you in good stead. I knew it was certainly not the environment for me, but I had no idea what lay beyond it or how to get there.

It hadn't always been like that.

I was like a butterfly on a dung heap Stella used to say, and I would laugh at the thought. But, as I became more and more fearful of my father and what he was capable of, I retreated into myself. Eventually, I was living a narrow, unfulfilled wreck of a life chained to my wretched home, miserable school days and enough crisps, chips and sweets to give me some comfort. Not only was I anti-social, increasingly hot-tempered and angry, but I was fat and so kids loved to taunt and bully me.

I was getting ready to blow.

As the door opened to Stella and Freddie's home, I looked at it as the crack I needed, just wide enough for a fat girl to squeeze through. Inside I knew I would find an entirely different world waiting to take me beyond my otherwise wretched daily life.

Every time I had visited it I had longed to stay and share it.

I knew now that it was meant for me.

It was how my life was meant to be but I had never known how to reach it. Then, today, my father went too far and, with one punch, sent me hurtling from Croydon to Epsom where, thank god, Stella and her family saved me.

Who knew that a black eye would change my life!

Forever.

3

A Second Chance

Edith's story...

I EXISTED IN A STATE OF shock and surreal uncertainty for a while, convinced that my luck wouldn't hold. Fearful that I would return to my old world without a map with which to make my escape; left to flounder blindly again and get nowhere. But that didn't seem to be happening. Stella and Freddie gave me a new home and Ronald gave me a new life, with a little help from Norma.

I loved my new room, my new home, my new neighbourhood, my new school, my new family and I was very afraid of losing it all. But I no longer had to worry about being hit - or worse - or trying to protect my mother, or wondering what trouble my loathsome brother was going to bestow upon our family.

I didn't have to worry about whether or not I would get hit at school, or teased, or humiliated. I knew I would get care, good food and, maybe, even a little bit of the love I had longed for.

Such simple needs for a fifteen-year-old.

I was given Norma's old room and a wardrobe still half full of her clothes. At eighteen, Norma had left her job working in the accounts department at a nearby factory and taken a beautician's course which led to several years at the BBC, working with famous and not so famous people, readying them for the lights and cameras.

At twenty-three she got the chance of a lifetime and went to work in the movie industry in Hollywood and never looked back. Can you imagine? Hollywood in the sixties, where life could be so glamorous, exciting and fun, but still safe. Where risks and recklessness didn't take you to the edge of despair like it would today. Mixing with the world's great stars, but mostly with the world's great, unknown, wannabe stars, Norma would return for vacations and regale us with telltale stories. She expurgated them enough to save Stella, who imagined danger on every street corner in Los Angeles, from a state of shock and constant anxiety.

But Norma was strong and determined.

She was going to make something of herself, either alone or by hitching up to someone who would help her do just that. I had seen her blossom from plain schoolgirl to a smart, worldly woman and I wanted some of that for myself.

The clothes left behind in her wardrobe were the clothes I most wanted to fit into and so I vowed to slim down enough to do just that. That became my goal.

To look gorgeous and curvy in lovely clothes. And I had a rack of them, free of charge and for the taking, in my room.

That was incentive enough.

"Hey, Edith, can I come in?" It was Ronnie at my bedroom door as I was gazing longingly at all those wonderful and exotic clothes. I was thrilled to see him again as it had been months since we had last seen each other. Now that he was living in London our paths rarely crossed.

"So, mum told me what's been going on with your mum and dad. How are you doing? I hate to say it but you look rough, and that bruise on your face isn't helping things."

"It's been a bloody awful time but Auntie Stella has been wonderful. I can't tell you how glad I am to be here. It's so, so different from my life at home. I just pinch myself every morning that I'm here and just hope I never have to leave."

"Well, that won't happen. At some point you're going to want to get out and go it alone." I must have looked disconcerted at the prospect. "Trust me, that day will happen even if you don't think it will." Ronnie moved over and sat on my bed, took my hand and smiled close to my face. "This is your home now, if you want it to be. You've had a shitty time and now you need to be able to make it better. We'll all help you do that and Mum most of all wants to see it because she feels so bad about your mother. She's really messed up your life so far, hasn't she? Now it's up to you to take charge and turn it into what you want it to be."

I started to cry.

"Oh, it's been so horrible! Look at me! Dressed like a slob; fat and ugly. I've got no friends. I get teased at school and hate myself, my life. Everything." I sobbed and turned to look him in the face, just inches away.

Ronnie was so lucky, I thought, and I told him so. He seemed to have such a perfect life - the antithesis of mine. Of course, I didn't realize at the time what was on the other side of the picture that I saw before me. All I saw was the perfect family home, the education, the friends and the good looks. Ronnie had stolen a little bit of Freddie's diluted Mediterranean bloodline and that had warmed his skin colour to an exotic shade of perpetual tan. He was taller than average, slim but sturdy, with a shock of soft, dark brown hair that constantly flopped forward boyishly.

You can imagine, can't you?

All that talk about 'the beautiful people' but, really, there weren't many beyond the rare few sixties swingers. The best of them were in America where the breeding stock was much, much better. Sadly, Britain was still a country of pale, half cooked people, topped off with bad hair, bad teeth and bodies ready for the rejects shelf, which meant that Ronnie had little competition. His simple, classic good looks, pools of greeny-blue eyes and a slight dimple in the chin made him an exotic breed in his own homeland.

I was always curious about what had gone wrong with the British. Had somebody pissed in the gene pool way back when and poisoned it?

"Ronnie, it's easy for you. You're so lucky!" I whined.

"Yes, I suppose I am lucky - now. But it wasn't always like this and it was never easy. It isn't easy now, but I have advantages. I'm lucky to have the parents I have and a great home to grow up in. You've had no luck on that score. But let me tell you something that will surprise you. Do you promise to keep what I tell you between you and me? Promise?"

"Yes, of course."

If Ronnie was going to confide in me, there was no way that I would ever break that trust.

"Do you know what a homosexual is?" he said slowly and deliberately, tipping his head slightly as he spoke.

"I think so. I've heard people talk about them, but never nice things. Friends on the estate talk about queers and poofs and shirt lifters. Are they the same thing?"

"Yes, and do you know what they do?"

"They're dirty old men is all I know, but I'm not sure what they do. To each other I mean. All I know is nobody seems to like them where I live. I mean lived. But I'm not sure they know why either."

"Well, let me tell you. Homosexuals are queers and poofs and shirt lifters, as your mates call them. But I don't care for any of those words if they're used by toe rags like them." Ronnie's voice was rising and he paused for a moment to calm it. "I prefer the new, nicer word - gay. They are gay, and even gays like being called gay, but we don't much like being called a poof, a fag, or a shirt lifter, quite honestly, unless we're saying it ourselves. Anyway, I'm one of those."

I think my eyes widened and my mouth went dry. "You are?" was all I could muster.

"Actually, there are hundreds and thousands and millions of us but we're invisible to most people. The only ones you know are the poor sods that your arsehole friends on the estate pick on."

Ronnie talked, opening up a whole new world to me. A world where outwardly normal people the world over behaved like normal people except for one thing; the men liked the men more than the women and the women liked the women more than the men. Not much to get excited about really, I thought, but Ronnie went on to explain what an emotionally charged subject this whole thing was.

"I hope I haven't overloaded you with this stuff," he said after he had explained it all to me as we sat on the bed, side by side.

"Well, it's a real eye-opener, but I can't really say I know what all the fuss would be about," I replied. "I mean it all seems pretty insignificant, doesn't it? Especially after you've seen how my family behave, and they're pretty typical."

"I totally agree, but you and I are in the tiny minority."

"I think love trumps hate any day, don't you? I asked. "Regardless of who it is you love. Or is that just a typical fifteen-year-old being naïve?"

"No, that's a typical fifteen-year-old being smart," Ronnie replied as he gave me a squeeze. "Me, I'm lucky because mum knows and Norma knows and they've accepted me for it and have been really supportive. Norma, of course, thinks it's really great to have a queer for a brother!" He laughed out loud. "Dad, I'm not sure. Mum has never told him but he never sees me bring home girlfriends and so he must wonder. Anyway, he never says anything and never asks. So long as mum's happy, he's happy. He can be a bit of a grumpy old sod and a bit of a stick in the mud so, honestly, I don't know if he'd disown me or just rip my heart out and throw it to the neighbour's dog. Quite honestly, I don't want to find out."

"Your father would never do that," I exclaimed. "He loves you too much. And, besides, Auntie Stella would kill him."

"Hmm. You'd be surprised what parents can do with something like this but, no, you're probably right. His heart's in the right place. He just wouldn't have a clue what to say or do. Except maybe pay a girl to give me a good time and sort me out."

We chuckled.

He put his arm around me and gave me a hug as he snuggled his head against mine. "So, that's my secret which I need you to keep, Edith. I want to share this with you because we're kindred spirits, you and me. We both know what it's like to be an outsider, but I can help you through that. Just as long as you keep it to yourself. Agreed?"

"Agreed."

"Let me ask you this? Have you ever gone to bed and never wanted to wake up again?"

I nodded.

"Woken up and wondered how you'd get through the day?"

I nodded.

"Wanted to run away and throw yourself over a cliff?"

I nodded again.

"Me too. I may look lucky to you. Outwardly, I have

everything that somebody like you would think I ought to have, to make me the luckiest person you could imagine. But don't forget that everybody's normal until you get to know them. And, now you know me, you know I'm far from normal and that comes with a bloody hefty price tag. Like suicide. I can tell you've obviously looked over that cliff too. Am I right?"

I nodded again and started to cry.

Ronnie was pulling the curtains away and I had nowhere to hide. I was facing my demons and my rescuer all at once and all I could do was mumble.

"It's been horrible but I don't want to talk about it. I'm just not ready."

I started to sob as a tidal wave of pent-up fear and pain suddenly seemed to break free and engulf me. I had never been in a safe place like this before where I could unravel my past and embrace the fallout without shame or embarrassment.

"Not pretty, is it? Trouble is, the view onto the rocks below is sometimes better than what's at the top of the cliff. I know. I've been there and made it back from the edge. You've been there too, I can tell. Now I have to help get ***you*** away from the edge as well."

I fumbled for the right words to say, but was simply too tongue-tied. This was all too raw and honest and I wasn't used to it.

"If we make it happen, then we'll make the best team ever," he exclaimed. "I'll show you a world you never knew existed. Whatever's happened, you can keep to yourself until you're ready to let it out but, when you do, it'll change your life. I recognise the pain. I've been there. I know it and I want to help." He hugged me tight. "Do you want your life to be changed in a way you never dreamed off? I think you do, don't you?"

I was bug-eyed, of course. "Yes, I want to change my

life; I want it so badly."

"That's good. All your life I've seen a good kid struggling to overcome all kinds of difficulties. You've never fitted in. That estate where you lived, where most of the people are beyond saving, and yet you didn't sink to their level. That's why you've been so miserable. Trapped in a place like that and not knowing how to get out. Well, now you're out and I'm going to see that you stay out and create a new life for yourself. Are you up for it?"

"More than anything! But I'm scared and I don't know where to start!" I cried.

"OK. So here's the plan. You're going to be my pet project. I'm young, handsome, intelligent, amusing, entertaining and you deserve some time with someone like me, don't you think?" Ronnie chuckled and put his nose to mine.

"Yes! Oh, Yes!"

I was so thrilled I could barely contain myself. I jumped off the bed and jumped and jumped in ecstasy before lunging at Ronnie and throwing my arms around him.

He held me and hugged me back. "That's more like the old Edith I used to know. I shouldn't be doing this. Being this close to a girl is bad for my image. What would my friends say if they saw us like this?" He winked and smiled and set me back on the bed next to him.

He was serious again. "The first thing you need to do is think about what you want to do next. What do you want to be? Where do you want to go and how do you want to get there? Then we need to put together a plan."

"Oh, god, I have no idea," I whined.

"Of course you don't. It's OK. Don't tell me now. Think about it, then write it down and we'll talk about it next weekend. I'll come down again for Sunday lunch and then we'll go for a walk and have a private chat - just you and me – and no busybody auntie Stella lurking about."

"You've got three months left in school and then you

have to decide if you want to go on and do "A" levels or whether you want to go to college for courses, or get a job. But don't forget, you need to think about where you want to end up years, even decades from now, and don't hold back. Dream a dream. Think about who you would most love to be. Read some books or magazines. Pick a person to be and reinvent yourself. And we'd better get back downstairs before Mum thinks I've gone all normal and grabbing a quick feel."

Suddenly I laughed.

I couldn't stop.

I felt light-headed.

This man had just ripped open the lid of the box I was squeezed into, desperate and stifling. I was emerging into a new place, a new world where everything that had been normal now seemed seedy and disgusting and everything that I had thought unattainable just might be within my grasp. Hot and pulsing, a new life seemed at the edge of my vision and I just wanted to get at it.

Now.

Breathless and heaving.

"Ronnie. You will help me get there, won't you?" I said before we went downstairs for tea.

"Of course I will! You just try and stop me."

So, that was how the plan began.

And Ronnie was unstoppable.

He took me under his wing, took control and groomed me into a whole new woman. And who better for the task than a cousin who happened to be gay, twenty-five years old and, against the odds, was now living a healthy, happy life in London.

He would know exactly what to make of me.

Of course, being queer in the sixties is almost unimaginable to anyone who's under forty today. It was a whole world away from being gay in the 21st century, where coming out today is likely to get you a promotion and elicit more sympathy, empathy and assistance than you can bear. Back then, I was to discover that there was not much 'coming out' and lots of being 'found out'. And being 'found out' as queer was like being 'found out' today as a paedophile.

It was incendiary – quite literally.

It engulfed families in flames.

It blew some apart.

Otherwise good, kind, generous people became apoplectic.

For far too many it exploded their worlds into a million tiny, ugly, damaging pieces, like shrapnel, that caused a great deal of grievous bodily and psychological harm. If you were not in a position to contain the damage, it could mean the end of your life as you knew it. Later, I was to see and hear about such lives destroyed and get to know the people who were still living in the ruins left behind.

That's why it was more about being found out than coming out. It meant telling lies and being furtive. But, it also meant being as carefree, wild and outrageous as you had the courage to be, within your own small circle - a circle tightly closed to outsiders and even to other gay people until they were able to discover the well-hidden key for themselves. One that gave them access to their own secret, safe little world.

Growing up, Ronnie was almost as quiet and shy as me. A real introvert he was, and never interested in sports, the boy scouts or other things that lads loved to do. Quiet, timid and rather studious as a child, he dared not be more than an apron string away from his mother. When I would visit with mum, he would play with me and help me dress my dolls.

Oh, the naiveté of children!

Although he was a teenager by then, he still couldn't

read the clues, and neither could I.

Eventually, we were to become each other's rock but, back then, we felt more like lumps of malleable putty, just waiting to be manhandled.

But that was then and now was different. Now he was a man, all confident and assured, although he had gotten there on shaky legs, running from shadows and hiding from ghosts.

After sorting himself out, Ronnie - bless him - was now concerned about me. He recognised a lost soul and an outsider, just like himself, fighting against the tide for survival, and so had all the sympathy in the world for me and my struggles. I was an outsider too, though I didn't know it back then. What I did know was that I didn't want to be like anybody I knew.

I would see the teenage girls, some barely out of school, pushing their prams and trapped for life. Or staggering out of the pubs with a new bloke on their arms, wondering whether to go all the way that night, or not.

I didn't want to be like any of them.

I recoiled from them.

And now I was free of it, surrounded, at last, by people who didn't have much of anything in common with those people either and much more in common with me.

Or so I hoped.

Ronnie had escaped too.

Surprisingly unscathed, he had avoided much of the damage that goes with accepting one's own homosexuality, but he had travelled long enough on the dark side of that lonely road to recognise a kindred spirit.

Working as an estate agent in Wimbledon, he shared a flat on Wimbledon Common, but he popped home frequently at weekends to see his family. He and Stella were close and, by this time, the apron string had stretched much further but had still not snapped. She was a free-thinker, modern in her ways and sympathetic in her emotions, so Ronnie had been able to disclose his deepest, darkest secret and experienced no hurt or rejection.

Spending time with Ronnie was a revelation about survival, love, passion, and drama but also humour. I loved the story of him and that's why I needed to tell it. Not just for him, or for me, but for others like him who, for whatever reason, had suffered for just being who they were.

And that would be an awful, awful lot of people.

Now he wanted to save my soul and I so needed a saviour.

Stella, thank God, was there for him. Struggling to make sense of what he was dealing with and where it might take him, her support and understanding were unique responses in those days and a generous contribution to his survival as a sound human being and, by osmosis, to my survival as well. Much as Stella worried about him and his future, she would fight all the gods and demons to protect him.

When Ronnie had told her she was shocked, as any mother would have been when discovering the wretched unknown.

But she said nothing.

No screaming fit.

No wailing.

No 'what have I done to deserve this?' and other equally unhelpful reactions. As Ronnie tells it, she simply said, quietly and calmly, 'I need a month to think about this, Ronnie.' And so began her task to find out everything she could about something she knew absolutely nothing about. Which as, it turned out, was about as much as most people knew; certainly the ones she knew.

She discovered it really was a love that dare not speak its name or tell anyone anything about it. Information was so hard to come by then but, in a month, she had learned enough to be able to sit down with Ronnie and talk about it intelligently and wisely.

I thought how amazing that was.

How many other mothers would have ever reacted in that way? So mature. So thoughtful and sensitive and wise. That was a mother you wanted to have on your side.

"I was blessed with my two children," Stella would say when mum and I had our occasional visits to see her. "And when I say blessed, I mean blessed."

My mother would shift in her seat.

Secretly, I think Stella delighted in her two children as well as loved them deeply. It amused her to tell friends about some, but not all, of their activities. She lived a big, wide, exciting life vicariously through them both.

Norma's letters home were juicy with Hollywood gossip and shenanigans. Through them, Stella learnt all about who was new and up and coming and who was on their way out. Stella lived a California lifestyle without ever going to America. Safe and sound at home, she discovered more than her friends and neighbours would ever know, or want to know.

"The things they get up to over there," she delighted in saying with a roundup of the latest scandal as we sat there bug-eyed and entranced. It was like learning about a parallel universe and only barely understanding the science.

Ronnie would roll his eyes and groan. "You think the same things don't go on over here?" he would say.

"Yes, but I don't hear about that, do I, Mr. Know-it-all?" she snipped back.

But she did.

In diluted form to avoid too much shock, she learnt from Ronnie about who lived on the outside of traditional society. Those who shrugged off the conventions of the time and just did what they had to do, while she herself played out her life in comfortable convention surrounded by suburban safety and security.

It was all too much for fathers like Freddie though, so it was best to keep him ignorant. He had raised two children in the best way he knew how, but it was Stella who would cherish them and guide them into adulthood, and now it was my turn to be nurtured by her and to grow, mature and - most importantly - flourish.

She'd always wanted another daughter, she often said.

Now she had one.

4

A Plan Unfolds

Edith's story...

A week later, true to his word, Ronnie was back for Sunday lunch. I had been euphoric all week. My head had spun constantly, like a whirlwind. The kids at school found me strange. Why? Because they found me happy and laughing; that's what was strange.

When had I done that before?

My few occasional friends asked me what was going on. I just smiled. All I could think about was what my new life might look like. The here and now were suddenly, and quite simply, completely and utterly irrelevant.

"It's such a beautiful day" said Stella as the last dishes were handed to her to go to the kitchen sink. "Freddie's going to take me out for the afternoon, aren't you Freddie? What are you both going to do? Ronnie, are you going to stay for tea? Edith has been cooped up in that school all week. Why don't you take her out for a walk on the heath?"

As Stella stood in the kitchen drying the dishes, I envied her this comfortable, suburban life, the likes of which I had never experienced before. She was happy and jolly - almost larger than life in her enjoyment of it.

Why couldn't my mother have ended up like that?

After all, it wasn't so difficult, was it?

Stella was all curves and soft roundness. Her face was round, her hazel eyes were large and round, her lips were full and always glowing red with freshly applied lipstick - her obsession - her bosom was ample and welcoming and her generous, curvaceous hips begged for a hug. Her black hair, still with only a hint of grey, was thick and full of soft, gentle waves. She was a handsome woman, enhanced by ample makeup. Not quite pretty but vivacious; her smile drawing people to her.

Like mother, like daughter I thought.

I could see where Norma had gotten the idea. Neither of them ever crossed the threshold without every hair in place, every brushstroke of mascara carefully applied, cheeks amply powdered and lipstick glowing like neon.

Whenever she could, Stella wore the tallest stiletto heels she could manage in order to show off her curvy calves. She was magnificent as she sailed through life like a boat's proud figurehead.

Their home was in a leafy, genteel suburb south of Epsom, not far from my home town of Croydon, but it felt a million miles away. Here the cheek by jowl nearness of human existence suddenly gave way to fields and farms and space to be alone or feel alone. Narrow, quiet roads, hedgerows, open space, the heath to walk on. It was all so desirable and I did desire it. I was sure it was what I was made for.

Or something even better.

But it had always been forbidden fruit.

Now, with all my thinking and reading, I was getting a hazy outline of what my new life could look like and it didn't look anything like the one I had left behind. I knew there were bigger and better things to come, but it was all so blurry, like an overexposed photograph.

"Yes, Edith and I will go for a walk, right Edith? Get you coat and let's go." Ronnie beamed across the table. "She's going to tell me all her secrets today and I'm going to tell her all mine."

Stella laughed loudly. "Not all of them I'm sure, Ronnie. She may not be able to handle so many shocks in one afternoon".

"Well, maybe not *all* of them" said Ronnie, winking at me.

He was right, of course, because some of them I knew already.

We left the house and strolled down the avenue towards the station, then veered off onto the heath and onto the footpaths. It was a beautiful early summer day, warm and luscious in the sun, which seemed to shine so much brighter now that I was away from the dreary concrete jungle that I had always considered so normal.

Ronnie chatted about his week in London and his work. Besides loving his job, he was so easy with people. They liked him, naturally. He put them at their ease and never talked down to them if they were NOCD – 'not our class, dear', nor did he grovel and fawn over the toffs. He was always just himself and the fact that he spoke well and looked good made it all the better.

It took me a while but, slowly, I came to realize that looking good, dressing well and being charming were the hallmarks of so many gay men. If a man was especially attractive, Ronnie would assure me that he was more than likely 'one of the boys'. Naturally, I disagreed until, time after time, he proved me wrong.

Why was that?

Did gay men get an extra dose of the beauty gene? Or did they just know how to use their natural gifts to advantage?

Ronnie regaled me with stories of his week. Clients he had dealt with. Couples he had shown homes to, some with husbands who had made slight and subtle passes at him. Husbands he had flirted gently with until he got a response which blinked green or red. The green light men he duly noted in his little black book for future reference.

It was a whole other world to me - that parallel universe again - but it was all fascinating and I loved to hear about it. Was this what they called the outside world? It seemed to me that he was having as much fun as any person had a right to while working. His territory at Wimbledon Common meant that he dealt with all types of people, but especially the moneyed class. Even in the sixties the Common was a desirable area and, while more expensive than most, it was nothing like the stratospheric prices that people would shake their heads at today.

The Common was also a hangout for homosexuals and Ronnie occasionally liked to hang out. As the months wore on and we talked more and more about more and more intimate things, I learnt all about this side of life. Somewhat repelled by its blatant sexuality but, nevertheless, intrigued by this other side of human nature, I absorbed his stories like a sponge. They enlightened me. They shook loose and set free the stiff and distorted bits of my self-righteous British sense of right and wrong that my own family's behaviour so far had not.

I also learnt that nothing turned a man on like the smell of sex. Helen Gurley Brown had said so. It was like a drug and I very quickly learnt that that weapon had to go into my arsenal if I was to get anywhere near where I wanted to go.

In the eyes of most women, men were pigs.

No matter at what level, they were too used to having everything their own way.

They were feral in their instincts and sexual needs.

They were dangerous, selfish and arrogant.

But thanks to the power of sex, as I quickly found out, they could be ensnared, re-trained and used to advantage. The good news was that they were usually too stupid to know they'd been had, at least until it was too late. All this Ronnie and I talked about endlessly over the months and years to come. But, today, they were the first pieces of my puzzle that were being put in place.

"So, have you given more thought to our chat last week?" asked Ronnie as we smiled and acknowledged other walkers out in the warm sunshine.

"I haven't thought about anything else, actually."

"And…?"

"Well, I read the newspapers, go to the library, and I've started to think - for myself, I mean. Maybe for the first time in my life and, guess what? I realise that I'm smarter than I thought."

"That's because you have - sorry, had – such a low opinion of yourself. We all knew that you had the spark in you, except your family tried to put it out. And now where do you want to go from here?"

"Have you heard of Helen Gurley Brown? I've been reading about her - she's wonderful. She's the sort of person who's going to change the world for women. She's - I don't know - different. She's like a different kind of woman. Like a different species - all new and modern and forward thinking. And another one is Mary Quant. She's extraordinary, don't you think?"

"I do," said Ronnie with a smug, sideways glance. "I've met her, you know."

"Have you really?"

"Yeah. At a party. I was there with a 'friend', who was a 'friend' of another 'friend' of hers. She was very hip. We only spoke for a few minutes. Everyone was after her that night. Flavour of the month. You could do a whole lot worse than end up like her, let me tell you. World at her feet and everything." Ronnie paused and turned to me quizzically. "So how do you propose to follow in the footsteps of Helen Gurley Brown or Mary Quant?"

"I'm not sure, but I know one thing and that's that I want to get out of school as quick as I bloody well can. I hate it. It's only the thought of leaving and making something of myself that'll get me through the next few months."

"And then what?"

We stopped at a clearing and looked across the open heath. It was lovely – clean, fresh and desirable - and a million miles away from where I had spent all my life until now. Sadly, it came at a price that I could not afford.

"I need to be rich," I said with a sigh as I stared out at the unattainable. "I need money. I need to stay out of where I came from and know I'll never go back."

"Who doesn't? But stick with me, kiddo. I'll get you there - if you're serious that is. Every smart woman needs a gay best friend. They're nothing without one, and don't let anyone tell you otherwise. Don't tell me that Helen or Mary don't have one; they probably have loads of them. We're what gives them that different perspective on life. You know, that 'savoir faire' to set themselves apart - same as we'll do for you."

"But how? I look like an old sack."

"Well, we are most certainly going to change all that, but first you have to be determined enough to want to do it. The name has to go. Sorry, but there ain't no future in being Edith Butt. You have to admit, it's not very sexy, is it? So, we have to pick a new name for you, and change it all legally if we have to."

He looked at me sharply as I muttered some uncertainty.

"Trust me," he said. "That name has got to go. You'll be re-christened and your life will change forever. Oh, and you have to lose thirty pounds." He laughed and hugged me to him as I groaned. "Thirty pounds have to go and then we can see what we're dealing with. What do you say to that?"

"I know I have to, but do I *really* have to?" I said and he looked at me sharply again. "Sorry, I meant *if* I have to then I will. I know I have to change, and I know I can't change looking like this."

"It'll be exciting! By the end of this summer we are going to transform you into a woman. You'll leave school a different person. Yes? That gives us three months to get you scaled down so that you can get into all those clothes that Norma has stuck in that closet of yours. You're both about the same height. Besides, you know mum's a whizz with the sewing machine, so she can make any alterations. And Norma's back this summer for a few months so she can help me redecorate you." He put his arm around my shoulder. "Is it a deal?"

We laughed and laughed and walked and talked and slowly the plan took shape. "Oooh, boy! I can hardly wait. We're going to turn you into the woman I've always wanted to be." Ronnie chuckled. "We're going to get photos of you done by David Bailey before this is all over, you'll see."

David Bailey? Wow. Even I knew who he was. Everyone knew who he was. The most iconic photographer of the young and trendy in that remarkable swinging sixties era. A magical success story that was, perhaps, never possible at any other time. Born in the East End of London and triumphant in his art, capturing the new and exotic faces of his time. Models that, for the very first time, became world famous in their own right. Twiggy, Jean Shrimpton, Penelope Tree.

Who remembers a model's name before the sixties?

It was all so radical.

And then marrying Catherine Deneuve, one of the sexiest film stars of that era. What a life! What a biography! What an epitaph! You can just imagine - 'Born poor.

Gave up rags for riches. Died happy.' Who knows about
the 'happy' but that was a life to think about.
For me to think about.
About what I had to do to make myself soar.

5

Edith Becomes Sophia

Edith's story...

And I did it.

I was transformed.

For three months, with the end of my schooldays now in sight, Stella took on the mission with passion. She set up a new diet for the whole family and everyone benefited from it. Stella and Freddie had put on weight over the years as they worked their way into comfortable middle age and we all vowed to get thinner together, but me especially.

Inch by inch we got smaller and more enthusiastic. Teachers and students at school started to notice me. I was happier, more talkative, more conspicuous, more confident. Small steps perhaps but, over those few months, I started my re-birth. Like waking from a long sleep that was more a nightmare than a dream, I began to feel like my old self again.

As I used to be years ago.

As the child I was.

Ronnie came over most weekends to visit and we talked and talked. He was as excited as I was with my progress and could see the makings of a whole new me. Or was it just the re-making of the old one, as I became confident and enthusiastic once again? We talked about names and what my new one should be? It had to be elegant, modern and sexy. After a lot of debate, we decided on Sophia. It stuck. As soon as I left school I used it everywhere and, eventually, it was made official.

More months passed and, just before school finished for me for ever, Ronnie took me for my first visit to a beauty salon - hair, makeup, the whole nine yards. It was a gift from Stella and Freddie. Stella had altered some of Norma's old clothes and also bought some new ones to fit my new, slimmer look.

This was to be my transformation day.

I took the train to Wimbledon and Ronnie met me at the station. I had never been there before. In fact, I had not been to many places before, and certainly not more than a few miles from the Croydon council flat that I had called home for most of my life. My world had been very, very small, grey and miserable. For too long I had just wanted to hide away from people and places. Now I was feeling almost ready to face the world, or at least my small, but increasingly larger, corner of it.

"Well that's looking better," said Ronnie, smiling, and giving me a peck on the cheek as we met at the station exit. "But I can tell that Mum helped you to choose these new duds."

"Why, what's wrong with them?"

"Nothing. They're nice. They're safe. They look like they were bought by someone who wanted to protect your virginity. But I think you need something a little bit more - how shall I put it – out there. You know - on the wild side, yeah?"

"I thought they looked nice," I replied, feeling totally deflated.

"Sophia, I'm sorry. I don't mean to be judgmental - critical, yes, but not judgmental. They look very nice but the world's changing. Clothes are going crazy and nice doesn't really cut it anymore. At least not if you want to stand out in a crowd and that's what this is all about, isn't it? Look at Carnaby Street! That's going to be our next stop after we get through today. You need a shot of psychedelic. We had a whip-round, your Mum as well, and I've got fifty quid here for us to spend today, all on you."

"Fifty quid!" I couldn't believe it. All added together, I'd never had that much money in my life before and I was going to spend it in one afternoon?

"We're going to go up to the Village and have some lunch. I'm starving. I had to work this morning and didn't have breakfast. Out late last night and spent too much. That's life in the city. It's so – *exciting*!" he whispered exuberantly. "Sometime soon you'll be having as much fun, only not in the same way. But then again maybe you will. I mean, we'll both be enjoying the pleasures of the flesh with young men of our choice, right?"

"Ronnie! You're making me blush. Don't forget I'm only sixteen. I shouldn't be talking about these things yet."

"Oh, don't be such a prude. Girls your age are getting knocked up all the time. I bet some of your classmates are doing it regularly. And besides, even if you're not doing it, you need to be talking about it. I think that's my next job once we've made you sexually desirable. We have to make sure you know how to use it and how not to."

"Ronnie!"

"Don't look at me like that. I'm deadly serious. You've got ambition and you're smart and, once we get you your good looks back, you're going to be very desirable, so you need to be prepared for the consequences."

"It's too soon for that."

"No it's not! I've been there already, so I know. You need to learn to have the upper hand - always." He wagged his finger at me and frowned like a concerned parent. "Now - lunch?"

We caught one of the familiar old red double-decker buses from the station up to the High Street, where we could stroll around the shops. The bus was filled with a microcosm of London life. You could see how society was unfolding just by riding this or any old London bus. There were old people in drab, worn clothes with pale, lined faces and dreadful hair.

They looked all chewed up and spat out.

But the young people! That was another story. Such a motley collection of styles in one generation - beards and long hair, bell-bottom pants and old army tops mixed with traditional, old-fashioned jackets and coats. Women with flowing manes, short skirts and lots of leg. Figure hugging jeans or long flowing wispy skirts, mingling alongside dreary, older women. Everywhere you looked the young were exploding with colour. Top of the Pops had just begun on TV and everything about being young was different from before. Everything except perhaps the angst that always went with being young.

Wimbledon High Street was a cozy, quiet shopping street in those days. Lively, yet relaxed. The people were interesting. It was a real mix of long-time residents and new executives living side by side in old Victorian houses on leafy streets, close to the great outdoors of the Common. It would be a few more years before I appreciated all the charms of the area to their fullest but, for now, it was all new, very different and very unattainable.

"Talk like them" said Ronnie.

"What?"

"Talk like them."

"Wotcha mean?"

"Exactly. Say wot doo you m-e-e-n. We have to get some plums in your mouth. Don't get me wrong, your accent isn't bad. It's just like a lot of others - and it's not cockney, thank god! But, if you're on your way up, you've got to talk 'toffee'." I looked at him quizzically. "You know, like a "toff". Hey, change of plan. We're not going to get lunch yet. We're going to grab a quick bite and then I'm taking you to the salon first thing. Charles will fit you in somewhere. He'll do anything for me." He grinned broadly and winked.

And off we went. Grabbing a sausage roll at the nearest bakery, we made a bee line for the salon. 'Great Expectations' it was called, which I thought was quite funny, in some charming old Dickensian building with a quaint old storefront behind which the dazzling bright lights and colours of the raging sixties were out in all their full, eye-popping glory.

All the young - and not so young - trendies were there in abundance for their weekend styling, getting ready for cocktail parties or bohemian soirees, late night discos or just a night out in the city, with a dream of meeting the perfect mate, or just the perfect lay.

It all looked so dazzling, so alien and I wanted to be a part of it, but something held me back.

Fear of the unknown?

"Do I really need to do all this?" I was rooted to the spot. "I hate to spend your parents' money on something so frivolous."

Ronnie stared at me in shock and horror.

"First of all, sweetheart, never *ever* underestimate the value of fabulous hair." Ronnie stood there disapprovingly, hands on hips, and I almost laughed, he looked so serious. "I'm not kidding. You have no idea what a difference this will make. You'll look back on this as the day that changed your life."

I beetled my brow ironically, an 'oh! please!' visibly stamped across it.

"It's like amazing sex. You don't need it but, boy, does it make you feel great. Seriously. I am not kidding. If you don't emerge a different person I, personally, will eat your underwear."

"Don't be so vulgar."

"Trust me, Sophia, I have no intention of chewing on your knickers. That's just how confident I am."

I turned again to gaze inside. "Is this like Vidal Sassoon?" I asked, as Ronnie pushed open the door.

"Yes, but a lot cheaper," Ronnie whispered before introducing me.

Ronnie made a beeline for a short, plump, grey-haired man who was waving his hands vigorously in all directions. "Charles, this is my not-yet-but-about-to-be, lovely cousin, Sophia. Charles, Sophia. Sophia, Charles - Charles Hickins. Hence, the name of the salon. Don't you think that's funny?" Ronnie grinned impishly.

"The pleasure is all yours, I'm sure," he cried with a beaming smile. "Ronnie told me you would be coming in today. Delighted to meet you and even more delighted when I see you go because, by then, you will be fabulous. I guarantee it." He paused and looked at me aghast. "But he didn't tell me there would be so much work to do!"

My face crumpled.

"Don't listen to him. He's just sour and bitter. You look a million dollars."

"Well, half a million. I'm going to add the other half." He smirked and arched his eyebrows. "Not a bad investment, wouldn't you say? But Ronald is right. Take no notice of me. I'm just a tired old queen, and Ronnie is my rent boy, you know." Charles paused for effect. "Oh, yes. Once a month he comes in and collects the rent for that beastly landlord that he manages this antique property for. The one who won't spend a penny on the place. He's probably made a fortune out of us over the years. Ronnie, you should marry him and set yourself up for life."

"I think Sophia would be more his type and, besides, what would become of you if I wasn't around to keep an eye on your best interests anymore?"

"Don't flatter yourself! You're not the only rent boy in town, you know." Charles sniped. "Now look at Sophia. She looks a bit troubled. Sophia, my dear this is just what we call 'gay banter.'" He whispered the last two words close to her ear, for discretion's sake, and then turned and winked at Ronnie. "Don't take any notice of me, sweetie. I'm old and jaded and before I get myself into more trouble, I'm going to find someone to take care of you. If you don't want to wait I have a nice little boy/girl who will amuse you and knows how to make the dullest girl look desirable. Or, if you can wait thirty minutes I have Natalie who can do almost as good a job but without the hysterics - if you get my drift."

"We'll wait for Natalie. I don't want to scare Sophia too much today." Ronnie leaned in close to Charles' face. "Meeting you is bad enough."

"I say nothing, Ronnie, dear. You come back in half an hour. Always a pleasure. Nice to meet you, Sophia. Come back soon!"

We stepped back into the High Street where Ronnie turned to me and laughed out loud. "Your face! You look completely stunned! I should have warned you but, if I did, it wouldn't have been half as much fun."

"I'm OK. Just a bit boggled. I've never known anything like this in my entire life and here it is just a few miles from where I grew up. I might as well have landed on another planet."

"This is nothing. You wait 'til we get you up to the city and open your eyes some more. So now we've got half an hour to kill and, look here, right next door we have a great-looking clothes store - just for you. Let's get started, shall we?"

So we did, and in half an hour I was all decked out, wearing the 'new me' look and carrying bags full of more life-changing clothes. It turned out to be a used clothes store, but one like no other I had ever seen before. Almost everything looked unused and, for a fraction of the price, I came out dressed for my new life four times over compared to the cost of new. Ronnie decided that, as I still had more weight to lose, there was no point wasting money on new clothes that might end up back in this same shop.

"You can come back in a couple of months, Sophe, and return them for re-sale and say in a loud voice 'Someone else might like these. They are just hanging off me now that I've lost so much weight'. The matrons will kill you and that heifer at the cash desk will explode."

I could barely walk out of the store.

The clothes I had worn were packed up and, in their place, I emerged with an orange mini-skirt accompanied by a loose chiffon blouse in multi-hues of orange, blue, red and yellow and, even though it was early summer, a pair of hardly used brown suede, knee-length boots. I don't think anyone, except my mother, had seen so much of my legs.

I was terrified.

Of something so inconsequential.

When I went into the store the worst part of me, I now realised, was everything I was wearing. But now it was just my head and, more specifically, my hair. It was all thanks to Ronnie. He was determined, confident, ruthless and made it crystal clear that I would have very little to say about it. And, yes, I was slowly learning the truth - every woman does, in fact, need at least one gay best friend to bring out their true potential. And to tell them the honest truth about how to do it.

"OK. The only thing missing now is confidence. When you emerge from that salon next door, you are going to need nerves of steel because you, missy, will have completed a total transformation since you got off that bus. But stick with me, kid, and we'll carry this off easy as pie."

He grabbed my shoulders, leaned in and stared straight into my eyes with an impish grin smeared across his face like chocolate on a fat kid's face.

"You're gonna turn heads on a street where heads are hard to turn, my girl. You mark my words."

"*Oh my gawd*!" That was Charles. "Would you look at her? What have you done to her, Ronnie, in just forty minutes? You're late for your appointment too, I noticed. But, you are most definitely forgiven. Listen up, everyone." He yelled to the whole salon. "Did anyone see a mousy little waif with this lovely young man here, not forty minutes ago? Did you? Did you?"

There was a small chorus of 'yeses' and a few 'no, but we noticed him'.

"Well, this is her. Back. Transformed." There were a few wolf whistles and shouts and cheers and I was mortified, utterly embarrassed and secretly thrilled. "Well, almost transformed," Charles added softly. "Now the rest is up to us." He turned and craned his neck around the room. "Natalie? Where are you dear? Come over her and finish the job. I can't wait to see how this movie ends. Ronnie, are you staying to supervise? But of course you are. Tony, get Mr. Moretti a coffee. No! A real coffee. You know, love, from beans."

Natalie came over and smiled. "Do you know what you want to do with your hair?" It was light brown, mousy, but with some highlights, she said, she could make it glow. "Who would you like to look like?"

"Twiggy" I said. "But I bet everyone says that, don't they?"

"Yeah, but most of them I discourage, including you. It might work for you and completely change you if that's what you want but I would recommend that you keep it longer and full and we'll help you give it body and thickness. You have a lovely round figure, Sophia, and a great bosom so we want something sexy to enhance that look. You know the Elizabeth Taylor and Marilyn Monroe waves are still a classic and, with all your curves, more suitable for you than the Twiggy look."

"Ronnie, what do you think?"

"Elizabeth Taylor sounds good to me. Your face is round enough and some highlights will bring out your blue eyes. I think it'll be great. You've got the tits for it!" Ronnie said with a wink. "Don't blush. You watch where men's eyes land after this little festival is over. But first put these on."

"Eyeshades?"

"Yes, you're only going to see the end result, not the process. We want this to be a complete surprise. You're not paying for this so you have no option," said Ronnie, as he slipped the shades gently over my eyes and led me, blindly, to my seat.

Half a terrifying hour later, I was led to another chair where I had to sit with my eyes closed as someone else took over to do my make-up before I was allowed to open my eyes. I gasped and then I cried. They were clever enough not to do too much to my eyes until the crying jag was over.

"Crying is common," said Tony as he came by with more coffee. "We always try and prepare for that. Crying could be bad as well as good, I'm afraid, but this is definitely good. Darling, you look fabulous with a capital WOW!"

I did.

It was true.

Just as Ronnie had predicted, I looked a million dollars but wouldn't have sold myself for the world. In fact, it didn't look anything like the 'me' I used to be. I stared into the mirror, transfixed, as Ronnie handed me the proof. He had brought an old photograph and everyone gathered around to exclaim over the amazing change. I stared and stared and stared and cried some more. I couldn't pull my eyes away from myself. I didn't want this moment to end and I was relieved that Ronnie would not have to eat my knickers.

"Thanks, Ronnie" was all I could say. "And thanks to all of you. You've changed my life," I added feebly, and meant it.

Ronnie, with a very smug look on his face, smiled at my reflection and took an exaggerated bow.

"Told you so."

My slightly over large, almond shaped eyes, which had not been my best feature, suddenly were. They made me look exotic. My rather pouty lips which, before, had made me look dour and unfriendly, now glossed to death, all of a sudden made me sexy, and my slightly over large nose now actually flattered my face. What they had done was an art form and I couldn't wait to see Norma again and get more lessons in this black magic.

I thought of the other Sophia, Sophia Loren, whose face was everywhere in the sixties with her unique combination of over-sized features. When taken together they flattered her face like no other, in an exotic way that few women could begin to approach.

She was an icon.

She was a superstar and it was all the result of nature, enhanced by cosmeticians.

Suddenly, I loved these people!

They finished off my eyes, once they had dried, and we stepped out into the early summer weather. I felt like a beautiful spy, looking lovely yet feeling I had to hide myself from everyone. I didn't have the courage yet to flaunt anything.

"You look marvellous, Sophe. You really do. I can't

believe it." Ronnie hugged me. "Now I'm going to show you off. Just wait 'til mum sees you - she'll have a stroke! Anyway, I'm starving, so let's have lunch. Let's go over there to 'The White Elephant'. We can get something to eat there and you won't get ogled to death at the same time. Not because you don't deserve it, but most of them are more likely to be ogling me, if you know what I mean. Not trying to steal your thunder, lovey, but you need time to get used to the stares and attention."

"Will they let me in? I'm underage."

"I know the management. They won't care as long as you keep off the booze. Besides, you don't look underage." He winked. "At least not today you don't."

We took a seat in a quiet corner with a window of obscured glass overlooking the street and I ordered a slim-line bitter lemon. Ronnie ordered a lager and lime and then we paused and thought about the last few momentous hours and the changes they had wrought for me.

"I still can't believe what just happened! Really, I'm a completely different person now. I know I look different but I can't believe how different I feel inside."

"Isn't it amazing what you can achieve for less than fifty quid when you know what you're doing? I mean, really. Think of Cinderella. Look what just a new pair of shoes did for her and imagine what all this can do for you!" Ronnie exclaimed, as he gave a sideways glance and a little wave to someone else behind me in the pub. He saw that I had seen. "Sorry. Just saw someone I know. There's a bit of a crowd that hang out here all of whom 'ride the same bus,' if you know what I mean, so it tends to get a bit social for me."

"Ride the same bus? What do you mean?" I said curiously.

"You know, like 'on the team', 'catch the same train' - men who like to be friendly with each other. I'm sorry, I shouldn't be exposing you to too much of this. I should have taken you somewhere else," he said, wrinkling his brow in a way that made him look so coy and lovable.

I beamed. "According to you, I'm a big girl now. All grown up. I need to start learning about the ways of the world. You know what I said all those weeks ago about who I would see myself as. I said Helen Gurley Brown or Mary Quant. I still think that. I've been doing more reading and the more I read the more I think about them. They are so modern! And now me too … I mean, look at me!"

"Sophia, you look terrific but I'm just a bit scared because I'm on my way to creating something - or someone - who's going to become confident enough to go anywhere she wants to go, and that's pretty powerful stuff. So now you *really* need to work out where this is going to take you. Have you?"

"Well, I don't want to go to University, even if I could. I never ever thought about that before, but these past few months I've become a changed person; swotting up and actually feeling intelligent. I might get some "O" levels this year but not enough to do much with. Besides, I couldn't stand to stay in school another two years! God! Just the thought of it ..."

At that moment the food arrived - a ham sandwich for me and cheese and pickle for Ronnie, accompanied by a bag of crisps. That was as good as pub fare got in the sixties and that was only if you were lucky. It really was all about the booze.

"Hello, Ronald, love," said the barmaid. "Don't often see you in 'ere of a Saturday afternoon. And with female company too. Things are changing, duck."

Ronnie laughed. "Not as much as you might think, Rita. This lovely girl that I have the privilege to be sitting next to is my cousin, Sophia. Sophia, this is Rita, the licensee's good wife."

Rita snorted. "Yeah, and the person what does all the work around 'ere and I ain't kiddin'," she yelled with a big belly laugh, loud enough for her husband to hear behind the bar. "Pleased to meet you, darlin'. If you're 'alf as nice as Ronald here, I hope to see you again. Gosh, you look lovely! You're all done up a treat, ain't she Stu?" Yelling across to her husband again.

"Thank you," I said shyly. I didn't know how to deal with this. It was all so new.

"Rita, look at this." Ronnie took the photo of me out of the envelope and showed it to her. "What do you think of this then? Sophia today," he said pointing his hand at me. "Sophia last Christmas."

"Bloody 'ell! I don't believe it! That's you, love, is it? I would never 'a guessed. You look completely and utterly different. Stu, come over 'ere and look at this."

Stu waddled over, a small man in height but mightily rotund in girth. Living off his own beer, I suspected.

"Hello, Ronnie. Hello love. Sofie is it?"

"No, Stu. It's Sophia. With a 'haich' " said Rita, clearly enjoying correcting Stu yet again. "Look at this lovely girl and then look at this photo. That's her. Before and after, ain't it?"

"Blimey. A bit like you, Rita, only the other way around," said Stu and roared with laughter.

"Oh, bugger off back to the bar, you daft sod." Rita frowned and pushed him back across the room.

"Lovely to meet you Sophia and you did the right thing, turning from that," he cried, waving a hand towards the photo, "into that," waving his hand at my face. "I know which I'd pick," Stu roared again with a big smile across his face "and it wouldn't be 'er," waving his hand this time at Rita.

"Oh, piss off," Rita yelled with disgust before switching faces and, with a wink and a beaming a smile, wished us "bone arpateet".

Ronnie winked at me and I giggled before munching on my sandwich. Rita was circling the floor, picking up dirty glasses and chatting to the other customers. She wasn't tall but she was voluptuous, bordering on fat. She had a low-cut dress on, showing the jiggly tops of her tits, just enough to titillate, without flaunting it.

She had a mass of peroxide blond curls and firm, shapely legs in high heels that generated a lot of hungry looks from the men there that preferred Rita over Ronnie. She had lots of everything, but the thing she had the most of was confidence. She was the queen of her castle, in her element and loving every minute of it.

Even I could see that.

"Sophe, you know what? As well as Helen what's her name and Mary Q, the other person you should try to be is Rita." He raised a hand against my look of surprise. "No, wait a minute. Look at her. I agree, you don't want to look like that or talk like that," he said quietly, "but she's got all the right ingredients. Trouble is she uses them to look cheap and tarty."

I looked at her again, but with a lot more attention this time and could see what Ronnie meant.

"Yes, you're right, she's got a certain something and she certainly gets attention."

"That's what sex looks like to the average hot-blooded male, Sophia, and probably smells like too, if you got close enough. If I have my way, you'll be getting the same, but classy. The one big thing she's got – besides the two other big things." He pressed his hands against his chest and raised them in an 'uplifting' motion, "is confidence. She's got it in spades and she's got them eating out of her hand. How else would they be able to sell their shitty food?" He sniggered. "That's what you need. But the most important thing is that you need to know how to use it. You, Sophia, need to spend some time as a barmaid!" Ronnie pointed his fork vigorously at me as he munched on his crisps and smiled.

6

Sampling the Sixties

Sophia's story...

And a barmaid I became, but not right away. I still had work to do. Over the months, Stella relished her role as mentor of the household food revolution. We all continued to lose weight. Even Freddie started to look more like his earlier slim, youthful self and started to take pride in his new appearance, taking up swimming again, walking more and grooming himself in a decidedly un-British way.

In my life I've realized that two of the greatest and rarest assets a British person can have - and this was especially true in the sixties and seventies - are great teeth and even greater hair. Stella and my mother had inherited both from their forebears and passed them on to their children and, as luck would have it, Freddie's distant continental genes had worked in his favour as well. As the new diet took hold, we evolved into sleeker, finer, healthier and more stylish versions of ourselves.

We bought new clothes. We ate more interesting and healthier meals. There was little choice in food then; it was a world away from the cornucopia available to us all now. Even cooking methods and habits in those days were guaranteed to provide underwhelming food and Stella made an effort to expand her repertoire, discovering new and inventive meals. She was always happy to experiment with ethnic foods which, in the sixties, rarely went beyond bad Chinese, and curry had barely left India.

We ventured forth on more, longer and brisker walks and generally thrived on our new way of life. Even Ronnie was impressed. He couldn't wait for Norma to come home for her summer visit and see her shock at the changes in all of us but, most of all, me.

We both took delight in the game and talked endlessly about what I would do when school finished, from being a plumber working for Freddie, to a model and everything in between.

"Can you imagine the wolf whistles you'd get every day," Freddie would tease. "Especially when you bend down to get under the sink. They'd all be standing in line to help you unblock your pipes."

"Fredd *–ie*! Don't be so vulgar! She's only a girl, for heaven's sake. You'll be scaring her away if you keep up that sort of talk. Take no notice, love." Stella would coo and give me her sweetest look while flinging daggers at Freddie.

"Well, you didn`t do so badly out of it," he would throw back at her and so the banter would continue, all fun and good nature, and so unlike my old home life that was now firmly behind me, the shadow lingering but fading.

Ronnie or Stella and I, and sometimes all three, spent numerous weekend afternoons hitting the High Streets - Oxford Street, Carnaby Street, the Kings Road; we saw them all and admired fashion after fashion as the new and wild styles evolved and were taken up.

What a time to be on the streets!

"Biba" had opened her store, where the young and trendy flocked to see and be seen, looking like a funeral in those dark 'maiden aunt' colours and smocks that they thrived on until the miniskirt exploded on the scene and raised mothers' eyebrows as high as the new hemlines. Along with the miniskirt came 'go-go' boots and 'kinky' boots to complete the outrageous new style.

Meanwhile, grandmothers were busy swooning as short hemlines was all it took to traumatise two whole generations of women at once. The dads and granddads, on the other hand, loved it. They hadn't seen so much lovely, soft, bare, young female flesh since their wedding night, and quite likely not even then.

In politics as well as fashion, London was the leading agent of change. The 'new left' movement, with its peaceful activism for social justice, gained ground while more and more people released their angry inner voices as the 'free speech' movement took off.

Ronnie loved that and was keen for the cause.

"Doesn't it make you mad?" he asked one evening when he was visiting to scrounge another free meal. "They give Martin Luther King the Nobel Peace Prize and then they assassinate Malcolm X."

"Who's Malcolm X?" I asked naively, as Freddie buried his nose in the newspaper and Stella washed up in the kitchen.

"Look at the front page of dad's paper. He's the Black Nationalist leader who was assassinated in America. And then they wonder why the Watts race riots break out in Los Angeles. It's caused a lot of fear. We've all been worried for Norma - mum especially - but, knowing her, she's kept well away from it."

"She knows how to take care of herself." Freddie mumbled behind his paper. "She's got more sense than to get involved with all that," he added.

Fatefully, as it turned out.

"And now the Black Panther Party has been formed and the negroes in America are mad as hell and who can blame them, having their rights shoved down their throats to choke on. At least in Britain life is a bit better than that for people like them." Ronnie was indignant now and wrinkled his brow. "You mark my words, the campaign against racial discrimination is gaining ground and I reckon the Race Relations Act is going to get passed sometime soon."

"They don't deserve it," said Freddie. "This isn't their country, after all."

"I can't believe you just said that. The fact that it's not their country is not the point. And anyway, they're here now so you could argue that it is. But discrimination is everywhere - then, now and for evermore - and something has to be done about it. People deserve their rights."

"At least we don't have the Vietnam War to deal with," I said to deflect the growing friction in the room.

He paused. "And don't get me going on that subject. It's despicable. They're targeting civilians as well as the military, did you know that? That's the first war ever to do that. It's disgusting, it's immoral and I'm sure it's illegal yet nobody stops it."

Freddie lowered his paper. "Be thankful you don't live there, my lad, or you'd be even more upset. You'd be in the army yourself and then see how you'd like it."

"I'd be a conchie."

"A what?" I asked naively.

"A conchie – a conscientious objector. There's not a chance in hell that I would be fighting to support those lying, cheating bastards running that country."

"Ronnie, language please," Stella cried from the kitchen.

Ronnie rolled his eyes.

"That's easy for you to say from thousands of miles away," Freddie replied sharply.

"Maybe, but you still wouldn't find me serving in it. And it's getting bigger and stronger and killing more and more people and all it is is a laboratory for new technology." He snapped back at Freddie. "Did you know they're developing ultrasensitive devices that could detect the enemy by heat, light and sound, not to mention cluster bombs, defoliants and napalm bombs that are killing and maiming thousands of innocent Vietnamese civilians."

"How do you know all this?" I asked.

"Because I've been reading all about it. It's shocking – not to mention immoral."

Ronnie was indignant and I admired him for his passion. I wondered if I would ever become passionate about a cause. Something worthwhile.

I did.

But not yet.

Despite the big, ugly, scary world that surrounded us, where women and children were dying horribly in a faraway land in ways and numbers that would eventually shame the world, we gleefully shopped our way through the streets of London. The brutality of the Vietnam War was gaining momentum on all fronts but, as yet, there was no anger and sorrow, except amongst the Vietnamese survivors who had no voice, no choice and no power except to stay and suffer.

In my own small world I was oblivious to it all, but it wouldn't always be that way.

In fact, the Vietnam War would change my life forever.

Until then though, our lives continued in the blissful ignorance of distracted youth. I was far more concerned and thrilled to discover that, with some fancy needlework by Stella, I had slimmed down sufficiently to start fitting into more and more of Norma's leftover clothes, than I was about napalm victims in Vietnam.

Scorched.

Scarred.

Destroyed.

But I was focused on other things because, by this time, I had emerged a stunner. It's difficult to explain but the combination of slimming, hairstyle, increasing confidence and physical maturity was the perfect storm of forces needed to completely re-invent myself.

My body was reaching its full potential.

Things that needed to grow had grown.

Things that needed to change had changed.

Gone was the chubby, shapeless body and, in its place, was the promise of a full-bodied, curvaceous, voluptuous woman determined to reach her zenith. The only difference was that I was now working hard to wring every last shred of advantage out of it. Ronnie would tell me over and over to never underestimate the value of fabulous hair. I always laughed at the apparent frivolity of it, but he was right. How could something so apparently mind-numbingly trivial, make so much difference?

But it did.

Because I was a woman.

And hair, after all is said and done, is a woman's crown.

I had spent my life like a jigsaw puzzle with too many missing parts, but at last they had been discovered and the whole stunning image was now complete. I had lifted myself up and out of the hole I had crawled into. The one I had created at the edge of the cliff that Ronnie had described so well. The one I might have chosen to jump off but hadn't. The one that was disappearing from view as I retreated, inch by inch, step by step, back towards the world I had inhabited safely, happily, even blissfully, as a child. Before everything had gone sour.

"Norma's coming home in two weeks for a month, Ronnie. Your mum told me this morning. She got a call from her at seven. We were all wondering who the bloody hell would be waking us up at that time on a Saturday morning, and nearly didn't answer. She's really excited."

"I bet," said Ronnie with a nod to a passing couple as we strolled down the King's Road one Saturday afternoon. "She will be absolutely ecstatic. I know mum would love to have Norma home again but she's going to have to make do with the occasional visit. Street riots or no street riots, I don't see her ever coming home. How is she? How's life in L.A.? I'm looking forward to getting the gossip from her on all that Hollywood intrigue. She's in makeup so I bet that's where the secrets get shared, don't you? All that bitchy backchat, who's sleeping with who. I can't wait."

"She's going to have a shock when she sees us all. We've all changed so much. All except you, that is, but then you were always way ahead of us to begin with," I said and smiled.

"Did you see that couple I nodded to just now, when they passed? Weren't they lovely? Did you notice?"

"No, sorry, I was too busy talking."

"Well, they're a story. Two of god's beautiful people. He plays on my team and she wanted a nice, safe, secure life so she married him. He keeps her in the style she wanted to become accustomed to and he never has to worry about being found out. He can play around and always have a happy, lovely housewife at home to be there for him and to hang on his arm whenever he needs to play the straight man. It's a great match, apparently. There's a quite a bit of it going on, you know. Marriage of convenience"

"What about her? You know – how does she get what she needs?"

"You mean, sex?" said Ronnie, raising an eyebrow at me.

"Well, yes. Or does he like women as well?"

"Maybe, but he probably lets her have the odd fling. Anyway, what do people want from marriage? Everybody wants different things and sometimes the strangest needs are satisfied when two apparently mismatched people get hitched."

"I suppose so. But my experience is based on who's going to raise the kids, cook the meals, do the cleaning and be a slave and who's going to be in the boozer every night, chase a bit of skirt, demand his wifely duties and how many times he has to hit her to keep her in line. That's my world."

My bile was rising.

The scarred memories were too recent.

"Well, you're not there anymore and that's certainly not my world, thank god. Scratch the surface of quite a few marriages and I'll guarantee you'll find quite a few queers lurking inside. It's a great place to hide, you know, all safe and sound. Have you seen the film "The Victim" with Dirk Bogarde?"

I shook my head.

"We have to go. It's fantastic. It's the first ever film to use the word '*h-o-m-o-s-e-x-u-a-l*' in it. Can you imagine? Dirk Bogarde plays a lawyer who was one and defended some others who were being blackmailed, just for being queer. He really stuck his neck out taking that role but he knew it needed to be done. So that people knew what was going on." Ronnie paused and turned away, frowning. "See what I mean about all the shit?" he sighed.

I nodded and changed the subject.

It was getting gloomy.

"I don't think women need it - sex I mean - as much as men, do they? But then how would I know! I don't even know what I'm supposed to do! Just the thought of it scares me to death. Maybe it does her too and she just enjoys being safe and protected. I bet lots of women would, if he was good to her."

"I wouldn't mind a nice, good looking man taking care of me, Sophe. Maybe we can find a nice one to look after both of us. What do you say? He can keep you in cars and clothes and he can keep me in bed. Maybe we could do threesomes?" He laughed and turned to stare in my eyes. "Wouldn't that be fun?"

"I don't think I like that idea," I exclaimed, half smiling. "Don't get me wrong - you're lovely an' all, but it would be like taking your clothes off in front of your brother - yucky! And, anyway, you shouldn't be talking like that to a sixteen-year-old girl. I'm not supposed to know any of that sort of thing, at least not yet. Besides, you'd be criticizing every lump and bump and curve and spot," I said, turning up my nose.

"No I wouldn't. You'd be lovely to hold. Look at you! Have you noticed men looking at you?"

I shook my head.

"Really? OK, I'll show you."

And we made our way through the busy streets of London, wandered through the shops, stopped at a coffee bar and, time after time, Ronnie would discreetly point a finger and say 'Eyeball alert' or 'Ogling to the left' or 'Ogling to the right' and I would turn slowly to try and catch their eye.

It was a game I became more and more confident at, but only when I was with Ronnie, so that I could do it safely with no chance of being pestered. Slowly, I would force myself to make eye contact. Only for a split second at first and then, over the weeks and months, I would lock onto the look and watch the response.

Some would look away embarrassed and some would hold it before letting go in a state of confusion. You could see what they were thinking – 'what just happened?' they said to themselves. But some would hold it and want to go in for the kill. Those I still worried about because they could spell trouble that I would not know how to handle.

But, in no time, it became addictive.

I started to realise, recognise and love the attention and it was like adrenalin pumped straight into my vital organs, making me tingle and glow. I can't tell you how much it helped my self-confidence, but I still couldn't do it alone. I still needed Ronnie there for safety but slowly, very slowly, even that slipped away and I was able to fly solo and deal with the vultures alone.

7

She Loves Me, Yeah, Yeah, Yeah

Ronnie's story...

Sophia's birthday was fast approaching and mum, dad and I decided that she deserved a real treat. She was doing a wonderful job of putting herself back together. Her confidence was returning, the light was back in her eyes - weaker than before - but, nevertheless, it was there and glowing brighter with each passing day.

When would it reach its full potential?

And would it eventually burst into flame?

Because what a looker she had already become!

She had always been a beautiful child, before she withered like a fading flower. Mum always thought it was from her and Evey's side of the family, but I knew it wasn't. Billy may have been an arsehole as a husband and a father but he was a hot looking arsehole.

Here's something I haven't told anyone.

I think I was in love with him from the moment a boy can do such a thing.

And he knew it.

But I didn't.

I think it fascinated him, having this girl - my mother's sister - hanging all over him and her prissy little teenage nephew with his tongue hanging out.

Was it that obvious?

Was *I* that obvious?

I must have been because one day, when he and Evey came to visit us, he came up to my bedroom when the women were working on lunch in the kitchen.

We made small talk.

Very small.

I could barely form the words when I was around him, he intimidated me so much with his animal attraction, his sexiness.

You could almost smell it.

I wanted to taste it but had no idea why.

He asked me what I was reading as his left hand nonchalantly stroked his crotch and awoke the sleeping beast just enough to catch my unswerving attention.

The trap had been sprung and - sucker that I was - I had been caught.

Like some lazy, snoozing animal I had walked right into it.

He smirked, then winked and whispered 'In your dreams' before turning around with a snicker and strolling back downstairs.

I could have died.

On the spot.

Right there.

DNR.

He'd figured me out long before I had myself. I came to realise that these things take time and, when it happened, I had only been the same age that Sophia was now. I used to have constant dreams of trying to unsuccessfully thread a big, thick piece of string through the great big eye of a great big needle and, no matter how hard I tried or how much I licked and stiffened the thread, it simply would not - never, ever - go through that fucking needle's eye. Two minutes with Freud would have sorted that out and saved me a lot of grief. Instead, it took me years.

Oh, boy!

Oh well.

That's why I thought that, pretty though Evey was as a mother, it was surely her father who had injected Sophia with the beauty gene. Those extra little things that turned pretty to alluring, sweet to sexy, were what Billy had. That's why he flaunted *'it'* and the girls all swooned. I was gratified to hear that the appeal was fading now, as he aged quickly and badly with too much beer and chips and no exercise.

Yes, I found that very gratifying.

Since the crotch rubbing episode I had avoided him at all costs, but I did have the satisfaction of knowing that, as his trajectory was plummeting, mine and his daughter's were very much on the rise.

To celebrate all these great achievements, we were taking Sophia to a concert for her birthday. Not just any concert but a Beatles concert on the other side of London at the Empire Pool in Wembley. Like millions of teenage girls around the world, Sophia was Beatles mad and we were going to indulge her.

But we were in a hurry.

And running late.

Mum was nearly hyperventilating by the time dad got home to take us.

"Jesus, Freddie. What time do you call this? We barely have enough time to get there. What were you thinking?"

"I couldn't help it, could I? Traffic was terrible and there's no telephone in my car last time I looked so I could call and tell you."

"There's no need to get snarky with me. It's not my fault you're late. Anyway, we'd better get our skates on. Quick."

Sophia and I looked at each other and grinned. Love isn't always pretty, I thought. But I knew all that bickering was love.

You can't buy that.

"Maybe we should drive up to Wimbledon and take the tube from there. It might be quicker than driving and then trying to park."

"If you think I'm going to walk in these heels, matey, you can think again."

"Well put some flat shoes on."

"Are you mad? Then I'd have to change my whole outfit."

"For a pair of shoes?" Freddie chided her.

"Oh, god. They don't understand women, do they Sophia?" Sophia was dressed far more sensibly in loon pants, a pair of flat-heeled boots and a duffle coat. It was May but the evening would be cool.

"You're dressed for a bloody dinner dance, Stella. Not a pop concert. Anyway, it's too late now. Let's go. I presume I'm driving all the way then?" Freddie asked wearily.

"Yes, you most certainly are. And don't get us lost or there'll be a murder tonight and it won't be a mystery."

Ah, the sweet words of love.

We were quickly on our way through suburbia and into the maze of London streets, along the edge of the city, to north London. The traffic was still bad. Everyone seemed to want to be out; all the London buses seemed to want to play in the traffic with all the taxis. It was slow going but we made it with minutes to spare.

"Give me the tickets. Stella."

"I haven't got the tickets, Freddie." The voice was acid. "You said you were bringing them."

"No I didn't. I said to you last night - make sure that you have the tickets in your purse."

"No you didn't."

"I did."

"No you didn't."

"YES, I bloody did."

Sophia was looking distressed so I said less than diplomatically, "Sod that. We don't bloody care who's supposed to have them. Will whoever's got them, just get them out."

I wasn't hysterical, but I was close, as was Sophia.

She had been dreaming of this night for weeks.

Mum and dad searched every pocket, every nook, every cranny and stared first at each other and then at us.

Mum spoke first.

Very quietly.

"Your dad's right. I remember him telling me now but I was busy finishing off some accounts and it completely slipped my mind. I was sure your dad was bringing them."

"So where are they?" I screamed as quietly as I could.

"They must be on the sideboard." Mum's face crumpled. "I'm so sorry."

We all looked at each other as if our worlds had ended and, for Sophia, it pretty much had - at least for that night.

She started to sob.

"How could you be so stupid?" she yelled. "You're as useless as my mother. How could you ruin my birthday like that?"

She ran off into the crowds and we all looked at each other as if we wanted someone dead.

"Stay here. Don't move. I'll try and find her. If I can't, then at least the three of us can join up again."

By now the crowds were thinning as everyone found their seats in the stadium, ready for the concert to begin. Soon it would be easy to spot a lost soul, suffering from misery and despair, lurking near one of the entrances with a look of longing and loss.

Suddenly, there was a roar from the crowds and a

panicked wave of stragglers pushed through the ticket gates. It was then that I saw her, kneeling on the ground with her head in her hands, a victim of the surge of lucky sods who could still get in.

I stopped and looked at her.

She looked so alone.

And vulnerable.

Still just a teenager with a life to live, new people to love and so many things to learn. For some strange reason the sight of her almost broke my heart, kneeling there.

Beaten down.

Again.

I walked up to her and put a hand on her shoulder. "I love you," I said, above the roar from inside. "And I want to give you a big hug." I reached out my hand and she looked up and sniffled, tears still running down her face.

"I love you too."

She reached for my hand and I lifted her up, all stained and muddy, and hugged her tight. "I love you, Sophe, but only in a brotherly way. It's OK. You're still safe." She squeezed me back.

And then, just at that moment, the Fab Four started their first song of the evening – "Can't buy me love, love, Can't buy me love ..."

"What perfect timing!" I shouted above the noise and held her close. Mum and dad had seen us as the forecourt emptied and they made their way tentatively towards us. Mum was visibly upset and wiping her eyes.

"I'm so, so sorry, sweetheart." She came within swiping distance of Sophia but she didn't throw a punch. "I'll make it up to you somehow."

Sophia smiled weakly and sniffled some more. "I think you probably have already, if I was honest."

"That's my girl."

That was dad. Good old dad. Always wanting to keep

everybody happy and always happier when they were, which is not easy sometimes with mum around.

"Oh, Sophia, I am sorry."

That was mum, all tearful and mournful. Good, kind mum. Prickly on the outside but a juicy, soft centre inside. She was crying now too, and hugging Sophia. "This was meant to be the best night out ever and I go and ruin it."

"What's done is done. You didn't do it intentionally."

That was dad again, as he gave mum a hug. We were all hugging and as I looked up I saw the bench. A lonely bench on the forecourt.

"Well, if we can't get in, let's sit down and listen to it here."

And that's what we did. It was hard and getting cold so we didn't stay for the whole concert but we did stay long enough to hear the echoing sounds of some of the world's most famous pop music, played live and in person by the most famous pop group that ever lived.

Sophia was expecting an evening in seventh heaven; she only achieved third or fourth. But it was still heaven alright as she sat there with her eyes closed, swaying and tapping to the music as I held her close, in a blanket of affection against the chill.

Songs like 'Drive My Car', 'Eight Days a Week', 'Eleanor Rigby', 'Please Please Me', 'I saw Her Standing There' and, of course, 'Can't Buy Me Love'. It seemed endless and forever as we sat there speechless and enthralled, not quite part of it all.

Yet there was something magical about being on a cold, hard bench on an empty, cheerless forecourt, in the dark, on a chilly evening, listening to the wailing of a group of mopheads, as our grannies called them, playing in front of a huge, near-hysterical crowd.

But mum wasn't dressed for it and, after about an hour, she started whining that she was cold and her high heels were killing her.

Silly cow.

"We told you to dress properly."

"I know, I know. It's all my fault the evening's ruined so I might as well do it properly and put us all out of our misery."

"The only misery around here is you," Dad snapped back. "But if you have to go, let's go. We'll stop at a 'Wimpy Bar' for a beefburger, shall we? That'll cheer us all up and we'll get away before the crowds."

So we did.

Wimpy burgers and chips for all.

Britain's answer to the hamburger way back then, and we all loved them. Just a fried meat patty of dubious origin, fried onions and lots of tomato sauce. Heaven! Our tastes were simple then, and so were the menus.

As we munched our way through our greasy meals, mum came up with another great idea for the next day to make up for the ruin of this one.

"Let's all go to Brighton tomorrow for the day. We'll drive down early. Take our time. The weather's nice. What d'you say?"

And so it was arranged for another family outing.

With a happier ending perhaps.

Or perhaps not.

8

Oh, I Do Like to be Beside the Seaside

Sophia's story...

We were tired by the time we got home. It had been an eventful evening and we were drained by the stress of it all. Without a word being said, we all made a beeline for the sideboard in the dining room and there, sitting proudly, were four tickets for the Beatles' concert.

We all sighed.

"I'd best throw those out, shall I?" Freddie asked softly. "Then we can forget all about it."

"No. I want to keep those. As a memento. I bet I'll have the only perfect original tickets from tonight."

"Thanks to you, Mum," snapped Ronnie.

"How many times do I have to say I'm sorry? I'm sorry! I'm sorry! Alright?"

I smiled, put my arm around her and gave her a squeeze. "It's OK. It was a lovely gift and we all ended up having fun after all, didn't we? And who knows, these tickets might be worth a lot one day."

"Tuck them away in your drawer then and make a wish. I'm off to bed," Stella said, stifling a yawn. "Night, night."

"I'll be right behind you, love. I'll just make sure everything's locked," replied Freddie before turning back to me. "Sorry about today, love. Hopefully, we can make it up to you tomorrow. We'll have a nice day out at the seaside, OK?"

"OK." I smiled. He was being sweet. I gave him a peck on the cheek. "Really. It's OK."

"Night then Sophia. Night, Ron. Don't tell your mother I said that. She hates me calling you Ron. But you're more of a Ron than a Ronald," he said with a chuckle.

Ronnie stared at me and gave me frantic hand signals. "Oh my god! What an evening! It couldn't have gone more wrong if we all planned it," he groaned. "At least he didn't say I'm more of a Rhonda to him than a Ronald!"

I started to laugh and in no time we were in hysterics and trying to stifle it so that they wouldn't hear us upstairs. "Never mind. Tomorrow is another day, they say. I'm sure it'll be better."

Well, it started off well enough.

Freddie wasn't a cook but, if there was one thing he knew how to do - and do well - it was a fry up, and that was his treat to us that day, getting up early and frying enough eggs, bacon, sausages, tomatoes and bread to feed an army. We all mumbled enthusiastically through full mouths, and meant it, before setting off stuffed and satisfied.

It was warm and sunny and portended a splendid day which, in many ways, it was. We took pleasure in the lovely drive through the countryside, stopping here and there to take in views or stretch our legs. It wasn't a long drive but the landscape was varied and interesting and everything looked fresh and clean in its new Spring clothes, especially as we were well away from the dinginess of London. Just seeing animals in fields was a treat, especially the lambs.

We made our way into town and parked at the Brighton seafront. Everyone was out strolling or sitting in deckchairs, on a sweet dairy high as they lapped up ice cream - their 'choc-ices', '99's' and 'Mivvi's'.

There were the lads, harmlessly chatting up the girls in the seafront pubs and coffee bars.

Then there were the mods.

Then the rockers.

Oh – oh!

Watch out!

Oil and water.

Everyone just got along, except them.

The sixties was the decade of hormone popping teenagers pitted one against the other in gang warfare - and what strange gangs. Mods on one side with their smart, shiny suits and ties, clean cut looks and short hair, driving scooters of all things, and not looking much like a gang at all.

Vespas and Lambrettas were their vehicles of choice as they tore around town, the boys looking vaguely like their girlfriends with a touch of makeup to finish off the look. There was even a scooter charge on Buckingham Palace and, as ludicrous as that might seem in hindsight, it led to them being branded subversive and dangerous.

The Rockers took a huge dislike to the Mods, considering these working-class yobs to be stuck up, pill-pushing, effeminate snobs with middle-class aspirations. Rockers preferred their motorbikes, leather jackets and Brylcreemed hair and decided to teach the Mods a lesson every chance they got. One of their favourite pastimes was to journey en-masse to some popular town, preferably a seaside town like Brighton, to do battle and create mayhem.

And that is just what happened as Ronnie and I

wandered through town after leaving Stella and Freddie on their deckchairs with their ice creams of choice, ensconced and happy for the afternoon. Ronnie and I, on the other hand, were ready for more excitement than that; but not as much as we got.

Nothing much was open, it being Sunday when, in Britain, nothing much of anything is open except the pubs and the chippies. As we strolled, a herd of beer-sodden rockers burst from one pub just as a herd of shandy-infused mods emerged from another. It was, of course, hate at first sight with us in the middle and nowhere to go.

No shops open.

No retreat.

Quick as a wink the charge was on and we were surrounded as they attacked each other. Ronnie grabbed my hand and dragged me down the street, pushing through the mods in what we hoped would be the line of least resistance.

We squeezed through the bulk of them and took a detour down the side of the pub that they had emerged from, hoping that would give us access to the next street and offer an escape from it all.

Mistake number one.

We ended up in the back yard of the pub where a few of the mods were still lurking, smoking a joint with their girlfriends and, by the time we had realized our mistake, we were in the middle of them.

"Well, well, well. What have we 'ere?" A tall, skinny yob with a magnificent eruption of acne had decided to take centre stage. "Can we 'elp you?"

"Can we get through here to the other street?" asked Ronnie in his politest English.

Mistake number two.

"You can if we let ya," he smiled. "You toffee-nosed git."

The rest of the group thought this was very amusing

and laughed uproariously as Ronnie pulled me again and turned to run back the way we had come.

Mistake number three.

We were surrounded now and the crowd was closing in. It looked as if they were - as they say in the movies - coming in for the kill.

"Oy, luv? Where did you pick up this poncy little twat from then, eh? He your boyfriend then, is he? You look too good for the likes of 'im," he shouted in full cockney volume for all to hear before turning to face Ronnie directly. "Besides, I'd say he'd rather bugger me than shag you, wouldn't you? Eh?"

He slid slowly towards Ronnie so that they were now just inches apart. He poked his finger repetitively into Ronnie's chest as he asked over and over.

"Well?"

Poke.

"Eh?"

Poke

"Eh?"

Poke.

"Eh?"

This was obviously considered hilariously witty repartee to all concerned except Ronnie and me, who were not sharing the joke nearly as well as they would have liked.

"Cat got your tongues, has it?" This from a skinny girl with short hair, cut like a boy's. "I bet he'd shag me though, wouldn't yer? Remind me of your boyfriend back 'ome, wouldn't it?"

Ronnie opened his mouth to speak.

Mistake number four.

Mistake number five would have been saying what he was about to say but was cut short by a smack in the head that Ronnie caught from the acne-clad yob. "Wanna fight, do yer? Stick up for yer honour in front of your so-called girlfriend?"

"Leave him alone. We've done nothing to you!" I was white with fury, trembling with fear and afraid that the fear was winning.

"Oy, hark at 'er. Her ladyship speaks and expects us to obey." He sneered, landing Ronnie another smack across the head and getting ready for another one. "You fuckin' poofter."

"Oy! What's going on out here?"

Thank god!

A policeman poked his head out of the back door of the pub and yelled.

Hooray for the men in blue.

I screamed. "Help! Please help us! They're beating up my boyfriend." But they were gone almost as quick as they had swarmed around us.

"Are you alright?"

"Yes, now that you're here. You saved our lives."

"Well, I'm glad you think so but they don't usually murder anybody. You'd have been safe enough if you don't mind a few bruises. You'd better come inside until this has all been cleared away. The coast is almost clear, although I'm not so sure about the seafront," he quipped mirthlessly. "Getting bloody sick to death with that lot. Bunch of tossers, the lot of them. I'd lock 'em all up and throw away the key, except we don't have enough room."

Ronnie and I slipped inside and took a seat in the half-empty pub which was, by now, clear of gang warfare and populated with worried-looking, middle-aged couples still stunned from the mayhem that they had just escaped.

I looked at Ronnie, who was sitting across a table from me with his head down. He was crying. Gentle, softly shifting movements that were as discreet as he could possibly make them, but he was crying alright and my white hot fury returned.

"Those fucking bastards," I said, the words even shocking

me, let alone the other nearby patrons who, despite their trauma, clearly disapproved of a girl swearing violently about as much as they disapproved of the thugs who had so terrified them.

I glared at them.

Fuck them all, I thought.

I went over to Ronnie's side of the table and put my arm around his shoulder. "I love you", I whispered and gave a watery laugh.

"Haven't we been here before?"

"Yes, yesterday."

"That's right. Only the tables are turned." He turned his red and watery eyes towards me. "I'm sorry that you're seeing me like this."

"Don't be silly. We're best mates and mates share this stuff." I hugged him a little more firmly. "You've seen me like this too."

"It's just that I feel so helpless sometimes. I should have been able to protect you, but I'm not sure I could have. And then when I hear people say things like that to my face, I feel so vulnerable. Am I that obvious?"

"Ronnie, they would have called their own dads queers if they knew it would get a rise out of them. They talk like morons and you talk like a grammar school boy and so that, automatically, makes you a poncy twat in their book. Of course they're going to have a go at you. On principle."

"Yes, I suppose you're right."

"Don't forget. I grew up around people like that. They were my neighbours. Some of them are nice but most of them are pigs, just like them. You shouldn't take any notice. They're not good enough to be shit on your shoe and don't you forget that. You're ten times the man they are."

"I'll take your word for it." Ronnie smiled wanly. "I suppose we should see if the coast is as clear as the policeman said it is, and make a run back to the beach and see if Mum and Dad are still alive.

"I'm not concerned about them. Your mum would have them all concussed with a swing of her handbag. And buried under five feet of sand."

"I'd like to see that," Ronnie sniffled, wiping his nose. He paused briefly and stared contemplatively into the thin air before adding, "You know, despite the shitty birthday weekend this turned out to be, it was quite a success really."

"Oh? How do you reckon that?"

"Well, I think we've gone from being just cousins to being best friends." He stared at me and smiled. "All in one weekend."

I reached out and squeezed his hand. "You know, I think you're right."

We both laughed and left. Sure enough, the coast was clear. Just like nothing had ever happened except for a few rubbish bins flipped over or tossed aside, spilling their contents all over the pavement.

Freddie and Stella were still in the same spot, but standing. Worrying. Sweeping the horizon for us and hoping that we were safe. I waved and Freddie spotted me and came running towards us.

"Ronnie! What happened?"

"It's OK, dad. It's just a scuff mark. We got caught in the fight."

"I can bloody see that. Jesus Christ! What a disaster. Your mother's going to be furious."

"I don't know why. It wasn't our fault."

"No! No! Not at you. With herself. That's two disasters she's caused in one weekend. She'll be hell to live with for weeks now. Shit. Here she comes ..."

But peace was quickly restored.

Stella swore she would never forgive herself, but she did. She swore we would never forgive her, but we did because, really, there was nothing to forgive. She swore

Ronnie would be scarred for life and she was right, but not in the way she meant because Ronnie received two wounds that day, I could tell. One outside and one inside. The cut healed quickly enough but the wound that wouldn't heal was the one to his own peace of mind - his soul.

That small scar was permanent.

9

The Return of the Prodigal Daughter

Sophia's story...

And then along came Norma.

She flew into Heathrow on a BOAC flight from Los Angeles and disembarked after a long, tiring journey looking like a million bucks. There were squeals all around. She tried hard to sound American but quickly slipped back into her entrenched English accent, but she looked American alright. That had most definitely changed forever.

Clearly determined to make an impression, she had dressed as differently as she possibly could from the typical English woman of her time, although that was becoming increasingly difficult as new fashion trends exploded everywhere. Trying hard to look so much like the thickly maned actresses she worked with daily, there was no escaping the fact that she was not a very pretty woman. I had never realized that before. The few times that I had seen her in recent years, her style had been thoroughly seductive and captivating but, now that I was getting wise to that trick, I could see beyond it to the rather plain woman underneath the façade. What it did show me was just how much that façade could achieve.

Even without any genuine good looks, her style turned heads at a time when so many people looked prematurely old, stale and dull. Her eyes were a bit too small and a little too close together. Her teeth pushed her mouth out slightly so that she seemed to be forever pouting, but perfectly applied makeup - her job after all - turned disadvantage to advantage. If I thought she looked great, she was overawed by how much I had changed.

"Ronald, did you do this? Did you turn our Edith from a girl into this woman? I didn't know you had it in you?" She let go of Stella and squeezed him tight. "Although I should have guessed."

"I helped as well you know," said Stella wanting some recognition too.

"I'm sure you did, and you look marvellous too, Mum. How much weight have you lost? A stone? More?" she said, as she put her arm around Stella's waist and we made our way through the terminal crowds. "It really shows."

"Well, thank god for that because I wouldn't want to go through all this giving up for nothing. Mind you, your father seems to like it because he's become more demanding recently, if you know what I mean. Mind you, he's become more fanciable too, so I'm not complaining." Stella giggled like a schoolgirl. "Who knows? You might have a little baby brother or sister to come home to."

"M-u-m! We don't need to know that!" cried Ronnie.

"Yes, you do! You all most definitely need to know that, because that's life and we all want to be wanted, don't we? Well - don't we? Besides, I got something extra out of it, didn't I Ronald? I got your dad to teach me to drive. But

I made it worth his while!" Stella gave us a big wink and we all sniggered; I was the only one to turn red.

"Where is dad anyway?" asked Norma, as we got closer to the exits.

"Oh, he's had to go into the office today, unexpectedly, but he's dying to see you. He'll be back in time for dinner so I'm driving you."

"Prepare for an experience." Ronnie rolled his eyes.

The drive home was uneventful, despite Stella insisting on turning around to talk to Norma, and despite the cries of "Mum! Watch where you're going - please…!"

We all tumbled out of the car and Norma went upstairs to unpack and tidy herself up.

I followed.

"Norma, can I come in?" I said, peeking around the door.

"Of course, luv! Take a pew," she said with as much forced aristocracy as she could muster. "I try and use this accent when I'm in L.A.. They love it. But look at you. I can't believe what you've turned into." Norma's smile dropped along with her voice. "Mum told me the whole story when she's been writing to me. I'm so sorry about what you've been through at home but it seems to have worked out for the best, hasn't it?"

"Your mum and dad have been wonderful and Ronnie, well, I can't say enough about what he's done. I've become his new hobby, I think. He's determined to turn me into a whole different person, come hell or high water and, honestly, I don't know what I would have done without him. He's really turned me inside out."

"Has he told you about himself?" Norma replied warily.

"You mean about how he's different from most other men? Sexually I mean."

"Obviously he has. That's good. It puts a whole new slant on how he behaves. I'm surrounded by them in California.

Lots of them keep it secret, some are more open about it and some completely flaunt it. It's so much fun some times. Ronnie always says that what every girl needs is a gay best friend and it's true. I've got a few friends out there who are homosexual, a few lesbians too for that matter, and a few who are couples, all living quite openly together as … as what? I'm not sure. Mates? I love it - it's so American. Anyway, what are your plans? Mum tells me that you've taken your O-levels and finished school and started a secretarial course this year, is that right?"

"Yes. Ronnie and I have talked a lot about it and he agrees that I should carry on with the secretarial thing and then maybe go to work for an estate agent and then see how it goes. It's not all a man's world anymore, he says, and with my tits I'd be a big hit with the husbands and their cheque books."

"You know what? He's bloody well right! Can you imagine? They would buy any bloody house you showed them if you pulled your neck line down far enough and smiled," laughed Norma. "And if they hesitate, just flash your tits!"

"I'm going to start working at 'The Golden Ewe' in a couple of weeks. You know, the pub at the end of the Parade, past the station. Just a couple of nights a week behind the bar. I told them a tiny white lie and said I was eighteen - well, I nearly am. Then I can practice my feminine skills in safety. What do you think?"

"I think it's a brilliant idea!"

Just at that moment Stella called up that tea was ready, so we went to join them downstairs and started talking all over again.

"So, Norma, anyone special in your life?" asked Ronnie loudly to get everyone's attention.

"W-e-l-l. There is somebody … " Norma smiled demurely.

"I knew it!" Ronnie cried. "You had a look about you that wasn't all false and artificial."

"Ha bloody ha." Norma scowled.

"Now, children…" Stella cried "Don't start this already, and stop being a pig, Ronald. Leave your sister alone. She hasn't been in ten minutes and you're already teasing her. Be nice, like you are with Sophia."

"I like the new name, by the way. Sophia is a whole world better than Edith," Norma exclaimed.

"Thank you. My point exactly," cried Ronnie. "Mark my words. It'll be the making of her. There aren't many stars named Edith."

"OK, enough," said Stella. "I want to know all about your mystery man, Norma."

And so the afternoon wore on. Everyone laughing and shouting, talking over each other, loving each other in their own special ways. I thought how completely and utterly different this was from the family life I had left behind. I didn't even know that families were supposed to be like this. Even the few friends I had at school didn't seem to have families anything like this one but, over the years, I realized that this was just another view of normal.

And we talked and talked and talked.

Freddie finally came home and we had a drink, then dinner and talked and talked and talked some more. But all the time we talked, only part of Ronnie was in the room. Over time, I understood why as I discovered more and more about what made Ronnie tick. How he lived his life. All parts of it, not just the parts that most people could tolerate. Even though it was the sixties and his mother and sister were tolerant, accepting Ronnie in every aspect of his life, it still felt more like tolerance and a lot less like acceptance.

Here was a good man, a kind man, partially locked away. Making the best of a hand dealt by fate, he was still one of the lucky ones. Living in a time of changing mores and ideas, of ever-increasing levels of evolution in music, fashion and sexual behaviour it was - finally and at long last - a better time to be oneself compared to the times that had gone before.

But still the stigma stuck.

Slowly, I unraveled the mystery of what being homosexual meant back then. It was, for the most part, being hidden away. Emerging carefully in safe surroundings and always aware that you might need to dive for cover from people who could be cruel, heartless and hateful if they chose to be.

Absolutely no-one was to be trusted because the fear of being outed or exposed was often enough to make one eat your own kind. There was no mercy and blackmail was a daily fear that people today can barely conceive of.

I wondered what would happen when Norma finds love and brings her boyfriend home to meet the family. There will be rejoicing. The fatted calf will be slaughtered, of course, and joyful celebrations will be enjoyed by all.

But what if Ronnie finds love? What drama and trauma will ensue from that? If he's lucky there will be some semblance of acceptance. If not, and if he's still lucky, it will hold for a while before the pressure of secrecy, deceits, inhibitions - all body blows to any successful relationship - shakes the whole damned thing apart.

When your family, the ones who gave you life and love and the genes that made you who you are, can't be trusted not to abandon you and turn you out, the very people who are supposed to be there for you no matter what, then who can you trust? I, for one, completely understood Ronnie's vulnerability, and that of others like him, because I already knew the treachery of family betrayal.

But, today, as we sat at the table and shared stories, I saw none of that. All I saw was a family having fun, laughing together and simply enjoying being reunited.

Norma's visit was a time to re-connect with her family and friends, and to impart some wisdom to me before I got myself into any trouble. She was bright, sharp and worldly and, as Stella would often say, had her head screwed on right. One warm evening, as we sat in the garden after dinner - just the two of us - she turned to me and quietly said "Has your mother seen you since you left?"

"No."

"Really? God, she'd have the shock of her life, seeing you now."

"I know. She wouldn't believe it, would she? I can't make up my mind whether to see her or just keep away."

"Well, that's your decision but I'd keep well away from that flat. See her on neutral ground if you're going to see her at all. You've made a lot of progress and you don't need anyone spoiling that. Look at me in L.A., moving to a new apartment beside a swimming pool and surrounded by lots of eligible single men. You can imagine the temptations that can lead to." She chuckled and winked at me. "God, Sophia, it's a world away from this place. I pinch myself sometimes just to remind me of how far I've gone and how different my world is. Now it's your turn," she said, looking directly at me. "And don't be afraid to go wherever you think you should go. Ignore the people who tell you otherwise."

"It's a bit scary though," I sighed. "I have no idea where all this is going to end up."

"Of course you don't! And, of course, you're scared! That's life. But if you have the right people to help you, you won't go wrong and Ronnie's one of the rightest ones there is." She tapped my hand with hers and whispered. "Stick close to him."

"If I have to chain us together, I will. He's not getting away from me."

"And I'll tell you someone else who's going to change the world for us women - Carl Djerassi. Ever heard of him?"

In total ignorance, I shook my head. "No reason why you would. He's the inventor of the birth control pill and that's going to do more to free women than just about anything that's gone before. And I'm telling you now you need to think about that."

"I do?"

"Of course you do. Ronnie tells me that you have plans. Plans to keep working your way out of that shitty place you called home until you came here. I reckon you know what you're doing, but you don't want to take any chances. You can have all the plans you want but, if you get pregnant, it's game over. Unless you're lucky enough to catch a big fish with a big bank account, but I wouldn't bet on that, at least not quickly. Too often they just run away before you can get the hook in. Are you a virgin?"

I wasn't sure whether to be shocked or embarrassed or both.

"It's OK, you can tell me. We're all in this together," said Norma, turning to me with a wry smile. "Sex is something that you're going to have to get used to at some stage. Doing it and talking about it. If you want me to guess, I'd say that you were still a virgin. My guess is that you haven't really realized that you've gone from turning boys off to turning them on, right?" She paused and laughed. "This is how we talk in America. That's what I love about it. They're so much more open about things. Well, most things anyway. That's why we got Helen Gurley Brown." Norma paused. "And Gloria Steinem and Betty Friedan, for that matter. But they don't like queers much. Oh no! No queers." She rolled her eyes. "So, are you still a virgin?"

I refused to acknowledge my father's previous assaults on me as anything sexual, just cruel, so I lied as best I could and hoped it didn't show. "Yes, I'm still a virgin. And I've never kissed a boy except a snog behind the gym with weedy Jimmy Flint from the flats across from mum and dad's. But that was nothing and he didn't even smell that nice. That's it, Norma, the extent of my experience," I laughed. "Except that's not experience, is it?"

Norma smiled, sipped her tea and faced the warmth of the dying sun. "Sex can be incredible, you know. Even for a woman. The trouble is that most men are so useless at it. They get all hot and excited they can barely control themselves and once you let them go all the way they're so desperate for it that it's all over in two minutes - if you're lucky - and we're all on our backs wondering when the fun's going to start."

I couldn't resist a laugh. She was being so brazen and bold. "Should I be taking notes?" I asked.

"Don't worry. You'll learn it all soon enough. But, honest to god, Sophia, you wonder what all the fuss is about and then, occasionally, you meet someone who knows what they're doing and it is sublime. It's like Guy Fawkes Night in your head when someone's thrown all the fireworks into the bonfire at once." She rolled her eyes. "Bang! What a sensation! But they're few and far between, let me tell you. If you can get one, don't lose him or, if you do, get another one just like him. They make life worth living, but the rest are just a waste of space."

Norma paused to light another cigarette and, puffing coolly from the side of her mouth, she leaned forward and whispered. "All this talk about women having great sex all the time and everywhere. Don't believe a word of it. They may be trying to find it, but they're not getting it. It's the sixties' myth, luv. Anyway, you'll be wanting to find out for yourself soon enough. Let me put it another way. A lot of young men are going to make you want to find out for yourself, but they'll only be into it for what they can get out of it. So, remember what I said, get on the pill and stay on the pill as soon as you think you might need it. You can always come off it for Mr. Right."

"To be honest, Norma, the idea of it scares me," I mumbled.

"What? The pill?

"No. Sex."

"Why? Everybody ends up doing it some time. Well nearly everybody. It's quite normal. There's no magic to it. Well, there is but that can come later." She paused. "Besides sex is where the power is. Always remember that. If you have that to offer, and they want it badly enough, you can get men to do just about anything."

"I don't really know what to do or anything, but I do know that the last thing I want is to be knocked up by some pimply teenage boy who can't think of anything else but getting his leg over and, when he does, I have to suffer the consequences with a baby to look after, and then another and another, and my life in ruins." I sighed. "I've seen it too many times where I grew up. 'Til death do us part - and most likely involving murder."

"What do you want?"

"Well, I know Ronnie thinks I can reach for the stars but that's not me. I'm not going to be another Mary Quant or Helen Gurley Brown. I just want to find some security and comfort - a lot like your mother has - and know that I don't have to worry where the next penny's coming from."

"You need a good husband then."

"Yes, I suppose I do."

"A good catch." She laughed. "Don't we all?"

We sat there and stared silently at the darkening sky before Norma stubbed out her cigarette and turned to me.

"But, first, I think we need to turn *you* into a good catch and I think sex should be the next part of your education, because the sexual revolution is most definitely underway and you do *not* want to be left behind. Especially if you want to snag a good man." Norma smiled. "And I know who's going to have fun with this when I'm gone. I'll see to that."

10

Sophia Hits the Town

Sophia's story...

Norma went back to Tinseltown and I set to work in the pub. Down the street, past the station and at the end of the shopping parade stood the ubiquitous, rather grand but shabby, suburban mock Tudor pub, set back from the road in a leafy car park. Built as part of the new social order that comes with urban sprawl, it had settled into quiet gentility as the focal point of the neighbourhood. No rowdies here, just a pleasant atmosphere, long before the days of lager louts and binge drinking.

Surrounded by pleasant streets of well-kept homes, where comfortably-off business men and professionals settled with their families, it was a haven of respectability, where the worst that could happen was a few extra drinks on someone's birthday with a few too many jovial and loud farewells. Broken glass, blood, curses and mayhem never visited this establishment.

Here I was safely able to see how the other half lived,

nicely separated by a strong, high bar that allowed me - and them - to keep their distance. I was able to hone my social skills, learn to enunciate, smile freely and, most importantly, flirt. This, I learnt, was a skill that needed a great deal of finesse.

Most customers had wives at home and so I needed to be familiar without being forward, friendly without being fresh. I didn't want to get men too interested in me or to give out too many wrong signals until I had learnt how to deal with the consequences. It was a fine line and I knew that learning how to walk it would save me. I also realized that this was the ideal environment to learn it.

By now, and much to my amazement, I was doing well at secretarial college, passing my exams with flying colours. Moving to Stella and Freddie's, and all the peace of mind that came with that, allowed me to stay clear-headed, focused and just get through it.

We all celebrated. Stella and Freddie paid for Ronnie to take me out for dinner, somewhere special. I was going to be initiated into the social mores of the wealthier urban classes and Ronnie was going to be my date.

He picked me up in the company car. These were still the days before company cars were common and this was *the* company car, or at least one of just a few. A fine new Rover, borrowed for the occasion. Of course, in the sixties it was the done thing to dress up formally for dinner in any good restaurant and so I was able to test the limits of my skills.

Ronnie arrived in a beautifully fitting dinner jacket, white shirt and bow tie, looking fabulous, and I was wearing a figure-hugging blue and white dress, cut low - but not too low - with a matching set of pearl necklace and earrings leant to me by Stella for the evening. A beautiful new pair of classic, navy blue, high-heeled shoes was a gift from Stella and Freddie, along with a trip to the hair stylist that afternoon.

I felt wonderful.

"You look fabulous!" cried Ronnie. "Doesn't she, Mum? Have you ever seen her look so good?" he said as he came across the living room and gave me a big hug. "Congratulations on the exam results. I knew you had it in you. Now the world's going to be your oyster and tonight you're going to take your first bite of it, so I really hope you like oysters".

"Ooh, how lovely," exclaimed Stella, feeling as excited as we were, even though she was not participating. "But don't do anything silly, Ronald. Remember she's barely out of school. She may look older but she's new to this, so you just take care of her."

"Yes, you keep her safe," said Freddie. "Take your eye off her for more than a minute and someone'll whisk her away, especially in that den of iniquity. But, blimey, Sophe, you look a million dollars. I wouldn't mind being seen with you on my arm tonight, honest to god I wouldn't. Even though you are my one and only, Stella," said Freddie turning and smiling sweetly at her.

"Don't turn on the charm with me, matey. It won't work because you're lousy at it," Stella replied and winked at me.

"OK. I have to shine tonight. This is as close to my coming out event as I'm ever going to get."

"Mine too," Ronnie smirked. "We should be going if we want to make Soho in time for our reservation. And we have to pick up Ellen and Peter first."

"Who are Ellen and Peter?" asked Stella. "You haven't mentioned them before."

"Yes, I have. They're just friends of mine and they're coming over to the flat and we're going from there. They're brother and sister. And don't be nosy." Ronnie smiled.

We finished our drinks and strolled out to the car. Tonight I was going to be able to put months of work to use and see how well I could carry it off. Working at the pub had given me much more confidence and working in the lounge bar had taught me how to chat easily with the husbands and the wives without making the wives jealous. Believe me, that was no mean feat and one that would prove an invaluable lesson well learnt.

The beautiful new car made its quiet, steady way to Wimbledon, through the smart new suburbs and into the shabbier, older neighbourhoods closer to the centre of London. We stopped at Ronnie's flat, on the third floor of a block of rent-controlled mansion flats managed by Ronnie's company. Despite our trips to Wimbledon together, I had never been there before and often wondered why I was never invited. It was a little faded, but the style and elegance of the building were clearly evident.

"What do you think?" asked Ronnie as we walked through the lobby and up the rather grand staircase clad in plush royal blue and gold carpet. The walls were a pale blue and, together, the effect was one of quiet good taste.

"It's lovely! How did you get it?"

"My company manages the building, so getting on the waiting list is one of the little perks of the job. Especially when it's rent controlled, which means it's cheap. Not bad, huh? The colours were my idea. I helped them choose. They couldn't make up their minds. That's where people like me are so useful. Come, Princess, take my arm and let's enter the lion's den!" Ronnie smiled and winked.

We entered the flat and I was in love.

I had never seen anything like it before. But, then again, I hadn't seen much of anything like this before, and said so. Raised in a council flat surrounded by blocks and blocks of more council flats, my neighbours had no taste and even less money. Stella and Freddie's house was a big step up, but this cool and contemporary style was something else again.

"Oh - WOW!" I exclaimed.

My jaw dropped.

I couldn't help it.

"It's like a magazine."

"You think so? It's nothing special. Most of it's from a great new store called 'Habitat'. I'll take you there one day. It's very contemporary - very Scandinavian! The rest of it's just stuff I've picked up in London."

"But it's the way it's all put together!" I whispered breathlessly.

"When god messed up with our genes he gave us queers good taste to compensate. That's why I told you - every woman needs to have at least one gay best friend," Ronnie laughed and moved us into the living room.

I inspected everything.

It was so different and modern.

Right down to the glasses and ashtrays.

"Can I live here?" I said pleadingly.

"No. Not yet anyway. But play your cards right and you'll have a husband who can buy you all of this and more."

"But he'd have to be gay, wouldn't he? I mean to do it right?"

"Possibly. Nothing wrong with that." Ronnie smirked. "As long as you get everything else you need on the side."

I was mesmerized. "I could stay here forever," I exclaimed and looked out of the window to the Common that I could see in the dim light of early evening, across the rooftops on the other side of the street. "You're so lucky," I cried.

"You think so? Yes, I suppose I am lucky - now. Or at least luckier. But the day I don't feel some fear in my life though, will be the day that I'm *really* happy."

"Fear in your life? What do you mean?" I was taken aback.

"I'm not going to spoil a good evening, especially when company's coming." There was a knock on the door. "Good timing," cried Ronnie. "That'll put a stop to the sob story. It can wait for later."

Ronnie strolled to the front door and ushered in the

guests. Ronnie hugged the woman and shook hands warmly with the man.

"Sophia, meet Ellen and Peter Devine. Don't be fooled by the name. They're brother and sister, not husband and wife."

"But we could be. Different fathers so we're less likely to breed crazy children. Although they tell me all children are crazy. Hello, Sophia, I'm Ellen, as I'm sure you guessed."

"And I'm Peter. And, my! Don't you look lovely! Ronnie told me that he had been busy creating you but I didn't realize he had such natural talent to work with already. But I have to say, Ronald, you have created a masterpiece! You're a proper little Henry Higgins."

I looked at him quizzically and blushed.

"As in 'My Fair Lady'?"

Ah, of course.

"Nice to meet you, Peter, and yes, Ronnie has worked wonders."

"I should say so," chimed Ellen.

Ellen was a slim, waifish wisp of a girl with bright blue eyes and lovely naturally blonde hair, cut in the style you might expect to see on a Pinnochio caricature; boyish, pert and pretty. Almost like a Twiggy clone, she was dressed in a slim fitting, black, knee-length dress and classic black high-heel shoes. She was naturally pretty, yet didn't really seem to know it.

Peter, on the other hand, was a little older and quite different. As her brother, he bore no similarities that you could point to. Tall and dark haired, rather studious in glasses, his round face and high cheek bones put him at odds with Ellen's origins. They smiled at each other often and were clearly fond of one another.

"Ronnie, I always like coming to this flat," said Peter. "It's always so bright and cheerful."

"And clean!" added Ellen. "It's such a treat to go to

someone's flat and actually see that they take pride in where they live." She paused. "I wish I could do it."

"Ronnie tells us that you're living with his parents. They must tell you all sorts of things about him that he wouldn't want us to know," said Ellen with a sly glance at Ronnie. "You must tell me some time when he can't get embarrassed or interrupt us," she added, smiling broadly in Ronnie's direction.

"She's very good at keeping secrets, aren't you, Sophia?" said Ronnie, looking me directly in the eye.

I just smiled.

"So how did you end up at his parent's house?" asked Peter.

Ronnie jumped in. "Sophia's parents were killed tragically in a car accident and so she came to live with us. It's been hard on you, hasn't it? Awful. But she's been able to get lots of love and support from my mother and father. My mother was Sophia's mother's sister so the bond is very close. And now she's trying to get her life back, aren't you Sophe?"

"Yes," was all I said.

Clearly Ronnie had a reason to tell this story and I was not going to get stuck in the middle of it until I knew why.

"That's so sad, Sophia," said Ellen, "but this is your very special night, so we're not going to dwell on that now and spoil your evening, right?"

"Well, we should get going if we're going to get to the restaurant on time," said Ronnie. "It's in Soho, so we'd better give ourselves plenty of time to get into the city. It's called "Amici". A very nice Italian restaurant. Mum chose it for dad's birthday last year and I think he was a bit shocked because it's quite modern and, of course, foreign food."

"What did he expect at an Italian restaurant?" asked Peter, rolling his eyes.

"A nice piece of beef." Ronnie rolled his eyes. "My father

may have Italian blood in him but he's British to the core."

"Well, I don't know about you, but I can't wait!" exclaimed Ellen. "I could eat Mount Vesuvius, I'm so hungry."

Ronnie drove us to Soho, wasting no time doing so. I had never eaten Italian food before, except for cans of 'Heinz' spaghetti, which I didn't think really counted for very much. In fact, I had hardly ever eaten at a restaurant before, except maybe the occasional visit to a 'Wimpy Bar'.

We chatted casually about inconsequential things as we made our way to the restaurant. I suppose that, being fairly new and in Soho, I should have expected something different, and it was. It was very modern in a casual way, with lots of bright colours and modern furniture behind a large plate glass window that dazzled with light. Through the windows you could already see that this was the place to be, with everyone decked out in their finest.

"Now this looks like fun," said Ellen, as she slipped through the front door.

And it was.

I was in awe.

We were shown to our table by a tall, dark, handsome waiter whose looks were not lost on Ronnie, or Peter for that matter. I wondered what he found so interesting. Like all the other waiters and waitresses, he was dressed in an open-necked shirt and black pants, covered with a big green apron, and looked every inch the authentic Italian waiter, but spoke more like Romford than Rome.

Many groomed heads turned our way that evening as we strolled through the restaurant.

"OK, well we're a bit of a floor show tonight, don't you think?" said Peter. "And they're not looking much at me. The rest of you are outshining everyone, especially you, Sophia."

We sat and wine was served. I shouldn't have been

drinking but I looked older than my teenage years, especially that night. I was trembling a little inside, but that eased quickly enough with the wine. It was cozy and warm and we quickly relaxed into easy conversation.

"So what are you going to do, Sophia, now that you've finished school. You must be what? Seventeen? Eighteen?" asked Peter. "You look a lot older and, frankly, if you don't mind me saying, you've got a body that most men - and some women I might add - would die for. Wouldn't you say, Ellen?"

"Look at this," said Ronnie, pulling that same old 'before' photograph of me out of his wallet. Once again I cringed. "This is Sophia when she came to live with mum and dad. I always like to carry it. Can you believe the transformation?"

Peter and Ellen glanced at the photo and then looked back and forth between me and it several times before speaking.

"I'm speechless and, believe me, that doesn't happen very often."

"I second that," Peter added, sipping his red wine.

"To be honest, this transformation has been a team effort," said Ronnie. "I can't take all the credit, although I will take most of it. All the family has helped but the biggest applause goes to Sophia for being such a great sport and sticking with it. Who would have thought that she had all those god-given benefits hidden away under all that fat and hair?" He stared back at the photograph with a look of mock surprise.

"Wow! That really is amazing. You have to do something with it. Take advantage of your natural gifts, I mean. You have a terrific future ahead of you, if you play the game right. Aren't I right, Peter? The world is a mysterious place, Sophia, and often not what it seems. You have to be ready to dive into the mysteries and take advantage of them. I mean, look at us. You, Sophia, are probably the most normal person at this table."

I looked at her quizzically, but I was willing to keep an open mind.

"I'm not kidding," Ellen exclaimed. "Ronnie enjoys the company of men. I enjoy the company of women and dearest, darling Peter here enjoys the company of both and, for some strange reason, I enjoy the company of Peter, even though he is my brother and of the wrong sex. But, I have to stress, not by the same father, so he is my half-brother, which makes it only slightly wicked. But you can appreciate the complications, can't you, and that's just at this one table!" Ellen exclaimed as loudly as possible while trying to avoid being overheard. "Look around this restaurant. There are so many lives being led that probably aren't anything like the stories you would imagine just by looking at these people."

By now we were eating our main course and we all took a moment to savour the flavours as I absorbed what Ellen had just said. My head, frankly, was spinning.

Did I hear her correctly?

Was I, in fact, eating dinner with a group of sexual deviants?

Would Ellen want to eat me next?

I laughed inwardly.

This was getting surreal.

"What did I tell you about life below the surface?" said Ronnie with a raised eyebrow. "But I think this might be a bit too much for a sweet teenager to take in all at once."

"Sorry, darling, but you just look so grown-up that I just think nothing much would shock you. But don't worry. We're all very civilised and safe to be around, despite what other people might say and think. But what do they know, for heaven's sake. Most people haven't got a clue about anything," she cried, taking a drag on her cigarette and a slurp of wine. "That pasta was delicious by the way. Absolutely delicious."

We had all finished our meals and we sat back and lit up. All except me that is. I was still curious and wanted to know more.

"So, Ellen, are you what they call a lesbian?" I said as quietly as I could while still being audible.

Ronnie smirked and stretched back in his seat. We had a quiet corner to ourselves and everyone seemed to want to talk. It was as if the whole world was peeling open layer by layer these days and tonight was time for yet more exfoliation.

"Yes, that's one word for people like me. Others are women with comfortable shoes and librarians. Code words so that we can talk in public. Things like 'do you think those women are librarians, dear? You know. Like us?' It's all quite funny and camp but very useful. And, yes, we're the other lot whose love dare not speak its name," she whispered stridently.

"Peter, on the other hand is fortunate to enjoy two loves that dare not speak their names, aren't you, Peter, my sweet?" Ellen blew cigarette smoke out of the corner of her mouth and smiled indulgently at her half-brother. "Incest and manplay. And he doesn't even look the type, does he? Sitting there all smart and conventional. Goes to show, Sophia, what goes on in the hearts of men - and women. But men especially, because they're all beasts. It's just that some are more beastly than others."

Peter leaned forward and took another cigarette from the packet of 'Oliver's' resting in the middle of the table, struck a match, inhaled and countered.

"We're not all beasts, Ellen. Not all of us. In fact, I've had some rather sweet ones in my time."

"Yes, Peter, they are all beasts. Some of them may have been nice to you while they knew they could get something they wanted from you, including money, I suspect." She flashed me a cock-eyed glance. "You see, Sophia dear, this is why you need to use your newly-discovered talents to advantage and go hunting. Kill some beasts. I suspect you don't know how to aim yet, let alone pull the trigger but, don't worry, darling, between the three of us we'll have you bagging trophies all over town."

"It sounds vaguely illegal and probably quite dangerous," I answered.

"Not at all! And besides, some of us are getting organized to take some of them down - all very legitimate. Some of us girls have started an organisation that we call '*LOVE*' – Ladies Organized for Values and Equality', except it's not really 'ladies', it's 'lezzies' - you know - lesbians. Except we wouldn't get very far using *that* word now would we?"

"That depends on how far you want to go and with whom," Peter quipped. "You'll meet lots of girlfriends."

"I'll meet lots of girlfriends with whatever name we use. You don't think a thing like that puts them off the scent, do you? Only the stupid heteros fall for that. Anyway, it doesn't really matter what you call it. The men are going to call you a lesbian whether you are or not, if you support a group like that."

"A group like what?" I asked.

"You know. Standing up for women's rights like abortion, birth control, freedom from domestic violence, equal pay - genital mutilation for rapists," she added with a wink. "We have meetings and town hall discussions. There are a lot of women who take this very seriously and, you mark my word, darling, change is coming." She wagged her finger vigorously at all of us in turn. "No matter how much the pigs squeal and shout. They don't understand what women want. All they want is for them to stay home and raise babies." Ellen's eyes were blazing as she leaned back in her chair and took a long drag on her cigarette. "Yuck! Perish the thought."

"As you can see, she takes this sort of stuff very seriously. Don't you, my sweet?"

"Too bloody right. Try and stop me. You should come to one of our meetings, Sophia. Find out more about it. If nothing else, you'll add some femininity to an otherwise plain group of women." Ellen grinned. "The pigs do have a point about the lezzies being a bit plain." She winked. "Anyway, Sophia, as I said, you should bag some trophies. You have god-given assets and, believe me, some men would kill to get their hands on them, so getting them to simply give you cash instead will be much, much easier. Without family, you need to protect yourself and there's nothing better than a big fat bank account to do that. Right, Peter?"

"Yes, sis, you're right. I mean, look at our family! Father is a surgeon. Mother is a spender. She came with nothing and now she has everything, thanks to dad. Mind you, so do we. Granddad was a 'Sir', on mothers' side, believe it or not. Dad always had money and he married for the blood line, so we've benefited, but mother especially. So, we've seen how this works firsthand."

"But what about you and Ellen?" I asked Peter.

"It's what they call brotherly love. Isn't it Ellen?" Peter smiled sweetly across the table, wine glass in hand. It was genuine affection, returned in Ellen's glance.

"Yes, my dear, and more." She stretched her hand across the table and gave Peter's a squeeze. "Don't ask me how it happened. It just did. Peter looked out for me when I was growing up and we were so close, weren't we, Peter? And one thing just led to another - and another, and another. But it's not exclusive. We share ourselves around. Peter with other boys and me, and sometimes even other girls, and vice versa occasionally - as the mood takes us." Ellen laughed. "It's surprisingly complicated."

"Yes, but we're very generous." Peter smirked. "We spread it around as much as we can."

"So, I'm sure I don't seem to be nearly as wicked as you thought I was, now that you've met these two far more wicked people," Ronnie said, smiling into his glass. He threw an admiring glance at the passing waiter and sighed. "Reminds me of a past love," he said, winking at us all.

"I never thought of you as wicked, and you know it. You're the best cousin a cousin could have," I said, now starting to feel the worse for wear after a couple of glasses of red wine that I was simply not used to drinking.

"So, Sophe, are you willing to have these two reprobates on your organizing committee? Because, if so, we can get to work on the next chapters of your life," said Ronnie, raising his glass.

"Yes!" I exclaimed, thrilled at the thought of so much alternative energy being directed at my cause.

"Right. Here's to Sophia, episode two!" he cried and we all clinked glasses.

"But on one condition" Ellen commanded. "You have to come to one of my ***LOVE*** meetings first."

And, under the influence of all that wine, I foolishly said yes.

We left the restaurant full of high spirits and good cheer, ready to change the world, at least until the influence of the alcohol wore off. As we turned the corner onto Soho Square I stopped in my tracks. Coming towards us was a crowd of chanting Hare Krishna devotees, all with shaved heads and dressed in pink robes.

They were almost ubiquitous on London streets in those days but I had never seen them before. They seemed so other-worldly, so extraordinary, so serene as they drifted past us with their lilting chant of 'hare Krishna – hare rana" and the cymbals jangling. Some of them gave us a sidelong smile as they went by.

I must have shown my surprise because Peter looked at me and roared. "If you could only see your face!"

"Is this London?" I asked and giggled before we all hooked arms and danced down the street chanting "hare Krishna – hare rana" and exploding with laughter.

I was beginning to see the point of alcohol.

If this is what it felt like, give me more.

11

My New Best Friend

Sophia's story...

SOON ENOUGH, THE SECOND CHAPTER OF my life began.

I completed my secretarial studies and worked a few evenings each week behind the bar. Every day I tried to imitate the classiest voices I had heard that day and would, consciously, try and enunciate just like them in the replies I made, whenever they talked to me.

As the months went by, my voice became more and more cultivated - exotic even - and throaty to the point that, as I got older, I became nick-named 'Deep Throat' after one of the first famous porn movies of the seventies, because it was sometimes so rich and smoky. Everyone thought the nickname hilarious, especially those who knew me well.

"You could seduce a blind man with that voice, Sophia," Ronnie used to say as the years went by. But, for now, I was happy to just listen and fine-tune my vocal chords.

I had made a few friends at secretarial college but, being

on a mission, I made a beeline for the ones who spoke BBC English and had their own cars, on the assumption that they had the money and influence to advance my cause. If that sounds cold and calculating, it's because that's precisely what it was.

But, most of all, I hung around Anita, who became my new best friend and seemed to have it all. All except the car anyway.

Anita captured my imagination. She was strong-willed and loud and, above all, she had confidence - oodles of it - and I was fascinated by her almost from the moment we met. She was not very tall but her willowy frame and long legs, with very little skirt to protect them from prying eyes, made her look taller than she was, not to mention attractive and exciting with that magnificent long mane of blonde hair. She had a 'devil-may-care-and-I-don't-give-a-damn' attitude that captivated me and many others besides. She collected admirers and hangers-on like some people collect stamps, but it was me that got special attention and I felt privileged - truly privileged. Little did I realise that I was her driving force more than she was mine.

Anita was a couple of years older than me. This wasn't much but, as teenagers, it was almost a world apart. I was in her thrall. Her enthusiasm and loud bohemian attitude was something I wanted to emulate. Frankly, I was surprised that she wanted to have anything to do with me but we clicked and, in no time, we were best friends and hanging around together both in college and out.

Anita had a voice that rang like a bell, loud and clear, and she had no intention of being overlooked or ignored. I think that was what intrigued me about her. Even though I had now emerged from my shell, I was a long way from developing the commanding presence that this girl seemed so naturally to have claimed. She was larger than life, louder than a church bell at midnight, and a bright canary yellow to the plain pale vanilla of me and everyone around me. If I couldn't be her, at the very least I wanted to be with her so that she would rub off on me.

She was old enough to drink, unlike me, but she would always manage to get us both into almost any pub, no questions asked. As she sat there, chain smoking and drinking beer alongside the best of them, she would flirt and tease her way through a surprising number of free drinks and, thanks to her, so did I.

Under her influence - and some of my own - I inched determinedly from under my insecurity blanket. I made an effort to look great every day and ingratiated myself with the right people. Boys followed me. Men admired me and not always from afar. I learnt to be assertive and how to give the inoffensive brush off which made them still want me - and often want me more - but put them at a suitable distance. I had seen Anita in action and, as I religiously followed her tips, I slowly discovered the art and science of how to be less of a house pet and more of an animal with acute survival instincts.

I wore tight-fitting sweaters and figure-hugging jeans, now all the rage. My bust looked magnificent in these outfits and I gained the confidence to show it off. I looked slightly bohemian but with all the style of the salon - hair always done beautifully, face always made up to look barely made up but highlighting every key element. I spent hours perfecting the craft after Norma's initiation rites. It was a lot of work, but it was a sound investment because now I really was becoming the star I wanted to be and, with every minute spent, I shone brighter.

We shone brighter.

On Saturdays we would go to the Top Rank or some other discotheque and dance ourselves to exhaustion to the amazing sounds of Tamla Motown or Merseyside, either dancing together - which we preferred - or with some older boys who might have caught our eye, or Anita's anyway.

No mistake, she was the leader of our two-girl pack and I was happy to follow as, over the weeks and months that followed, Anita and I became practically joined at the hip. More and more I would invite her over to Stella and Freddie's, where we would spend hours in my room. We listened to 'Beatles' records over and over again, talking tirelessly about how we wanted our lives to be; daydreaming about what it would be like to be the wife of any of the 'Fab Four'.

Stella, however, wasn't quite as enthusiastic about our friendship as I was, but then I was young, innocent and naïve. She laughed as loud as anyone when Anita told outrageous stories about her aristocratic parents and their numerous sycophantic hangers-on, her alcoholic brother, her lesbian aunt and a whole host of eccentric relatives bouncing around their stately homes.

"You want to watch that one," Stella said quietly after I had closed the front door on another night of partying with Anita that involved just a few too many drinks and cigarettes.

"What do you mean?" I asked vacantly, my head still floating several inches above my body, as I followed Stella into the kitchen. She was ready for bed, enfolded in a thick pink dressing gown and hair curlers carefully planted symmetrically across her head. She looked vaguely ridiculous and I stifled an alcohol-induced giggle.

"What I say. You want to watch that one. She's very lively and funny but she's going to get you into trouble if you're not careful."

"Why would you say that? Just because she's young and pretty and lots of laughs? I thought you would be happy for me to have a good friend."

"I want you to have a good friend. I can't think of anything better for you than a good friend but I don't think she's going to be a ***good*** friend for you in the long run."

I foolishly - and drunkenly - took a step too far.

"You're only saying that because you're jealous."

"Why would I be jealous of her?"

"Because she's young and pretty and you're not."

Even in my drunken haze I could tell I had stepped over the edge. I saw her body stiffen and so I made a quick dive to save the night.

"I mean you were but now you're not."

Ooops. That wasn't what I meant.

"I mean you are but now you're older."

Stella put her hands on her hips and glared. "And you are drinking too much, my girl. You're not even legal. If that's not being a bad influence, then I don't know what is. You wouldn't be doing this if it wasn't for her."

My bravado was fragile and it shriveled under the harsh glare of those eyes. She relented.

"Look. Go to bed and we'll talk about this again in the morning."

I slept fitfully and fought against the drunken swirling in my head that jolted me awake numerous times as my brain spun me close to vomiting, which eventually I did. All over the pillows and even on the carpet as I struggled to get upright and out of bed.

My head throbbed and I cried quietly as I wallowed in my own self-induced misery. But nobody stirred as I cleaned myself, and my bed, up as best I could and waited for Saturday morning to take hold.

I rose late from my stained and smelly bed with a hangover the likes of which I had never experienced before. Not that I had had a lot to drink but I wasn't used to it. The mix had been lethal as I sampled my way around the contents of the bar.

Stella was busy in the kitchen.

"Good morning," she said stiffly as I crept down the stairs, dreading the fallout from last night. "I imagine you would like a cup of strong coffee, would you?"

I mumbled my acknowledgement as I slipped into the kitchen to face her.

"That bedroom must be a nasty mess this morning, based on the noises I heard last night."

I burst into tears. "I'm sorry. I feel awful and my head hurts so bad."

Stella snorted. "You'd better get used to that, my girl. Like it or not that won't be the last time you feel like this. Even the best of us fall under the influence sometimes." She folded her arms and stared at me, but her look softened. "You look like a war zone! Go into the sitting room and I'll bring you a mug of hot, strong coffee. And then you can clean up your mess because you're on your own with that one."

I slipped quietly into the lounge, sat down and waited. I couldn't recall what I had said to Stella last night but I knew that words were spoken which I would now regret.

Stella appeared with two mugs of coffee and sat down across from me.

"Every now and again I love a good cup of coffee but it's so hard to find good coffee."

She sat. She stared.

"I'm sorry about last night," I mumbled.

"Which part?"

I looked at her quizzically.

"The getting sick, the getting drunk, the being rude, or all three?"

"Well, all three I suppose. I can't remember what I said but I think I was rude to you, wasn't I?"

"Not really. It's the fact that you were drunk in the first place that upset me." She sipped her coffee and stared out of the window. "I know you really like this Anita girl but you really have to be careful. I'm a lot older than you - as you very clearly pointed out to me last night - but I've seen a lot more of life than you have and been let down by a lot more people than you have ever had a chance to meet yet and, in my opinion, Anita is one of those."

I opened my mouth to say something in her defence but Stella ruthlessly cut me off.

"Hear me out first. She tells all these stories about her family and all the exciting things she does with them. All the people that they - supposedly - know. But have you ever met any of them? Been to her house?"

I shook my head.

"Do you even know where she lives?"

Again, I shook my head.

"I'm not trying to be a fly in the ointment here, but she worries me. You're still young and impressionable; so is she for that matter. But she's strong-willed and hot-headed. If she goes down she'll drag you down with her, only she won't care and you will." She gave me a sympathetic smile. "Believe me. I've met girls like this before. I was young myself, believe it or not, and they can be very dangerous."

I swallowed my coffee but it didn't help with my condition as I sat there and took in Stella's words of advice as well as my sad, dopey, dizzy head would allow.

She was right of course.

Since I had met Anita I had been charmed and disarmed but Stella's well-meaning advice had rattled me. I started to be more aware of Anita and to question, although reluctantly, everything she said and to not treat it as gospel just because she said so.

I began to notice how much she avoided any suggestion to meet her family. She was absolutely not having any of that and so one evening after class I followed her home. It wasn't easy slipping undetected onto the same tube train as we parted at Putney Bridge station, but I did it. I had borrowed a scarf and a pair of dark glasses from Stella and surreptitiously slipped them on for some anonymity.

At Earl's Court station she hopped out of her seat at the last minute before the doors closed, as if her mind had been completely in another world. I only just managed to get out in time to avoid losing her, just as the train started to move.

She walked briskly for several minutes before turning away from the main road. All of a sudden, I found myself following her into what appeared to be an entirely different world of sad and crumby old Victorian houses and poorly converted flats. They almost made my dreary childhood council flat home appear positively grand.

About halfway along the road she pulled out her key, inserted it in the lock of the front door of probably the most dilapidated house in the street and disappeared inside.

12

Out of My Depth

Sophia's story...

It wasn't long before Anita's behaviour became more and more erratic. She would fly as high as a kite and want to do the most outrageous things - and often did. After weekends when we hadn't seen each other, she would often return to college on Monday morning and flash a new piece of jewelry that she claimed had been bought for her by her mother or father or some other close relative.

But never a boyfriend.

She disdained boyfriends.

Boyfriends never seemed to enter her life and I had often looked on amazed as she crushed her admirers in a way that I would never have had the courage to do. With just a few sharp words she left them speechless, their balls shrivelled to the size of raisins, and she did it without ever using the 'F' word. In hindsight, I consider that to have been a remarkable feat. She was proving to be a conundrum alright.

Then, one weekend, it all went horribly wrong and the charade was over.

Anita wanted to go to a dinner dance in the City. Apparently, there would be a few celebrities there and she had gotten tickets from a wealthy cousin and wanted someone to tag along with her. Naturally, I was quite excited and gave her a resounding, if foolish, yes.

The week before the event she and I had gone window shopping in town and daydreamed about new outfits to wear to this supposedly grand affair - you know the way girls do.

"It's alright for you," I said. "Your mother will buy you whatever you want."

"In my dreams!" she snapped back before regaining her composure and 'oohing' and 'aahing' at the jewelry in the shop window that we were standing in front of. "Let's go in and have a look, shall we? Maybe I'll see something that I can have put aside. Daddy can pay for it later."

In we strolled, Anita more confident than Eartha Kitt before an adoring audience of thousands and, dressed to the nines, she looked every bit the socialite she claimed to be. Without all of Anita's gold and glitter, I looked more like the next best thing.

It didn't take long before the shop assistants were eating out of her hands. She had them trapped and helpless in that magical web that had previously claimed me. As I saw her slip a pair of earrings and a necklace into her purse while she had them nicely distracted, I realised that this was all a game to her; this fantasy that she conjured up to beguile and entrap, use and dispose. I was just another pawn in that game, although I was clearly still useful in some way. She still seemed to want me around for some reason I had not quite figured out, when she had a whole coterie vying for her attention.

Anita made a loud noise about having to dash away

for an appointment and could they put aside a beautiful diamond bracelet that her father would pick up and pay for the following week. Naively they took down the particulars and assured her that it would be wrapped and ready as we bustled out of the door. It was that easy. But it took a pro to pull it off and, as it turned out, a pro is what she was.

With the jewelry safely stashed away, off we went to join the hordes of young women hunting every corner of 'Biba', the mecca for all things new in fashion before zooming off to the Kings Road for another hunt for the new and different at 'Granny Takes a Trip'. It all seems so predictable now but seemed so much fun at the time.

I didn't say anything about what I had seen her do until the evening of the dinner dance. She assured me that the event would be very proper and I had echoed that to Stella, but she had her doubts simply because Anita was involved.

The event was held in a small but quite exclusive private club in the West End and everyone was dressed to the nines. I had never attended anything like this before so I didn't think it strange that there were gambling tables everywhere. Around them people were eagerly following the roll of a dice or the spin of a wheel, anticipating a win that might change their lives, but never enjoying one.

The look of anxious expectation was new to me but I recognised it immediately for what it was. Despite my lack of worldliness, I wasn't entirely at ease as we both swanned through the elegant club, turned heads bobbing in our wake. Individually, we looked splendid but, together, we really put on a show.

Anita stopped at a table not far from the bar and introduced me to two almost handsome, well-dressed men already sitting there. They were youthful but not young, probably in their late thirties, and both looked remarkably alike, which made sense as they turned out to be brothers. Twins in fact.

They made me uneasy.

I was young and naïve but even I could recognise malevolence when I saw it.

"Sophia, this is Eddie," she said bending over and exchanging lip kisses with him. "And this is Charles." She leaned over and gave him a peck on the cheek. "And never call him Charlie. He hates it." She giggled loudly and I could see her whole body gearing up into star attraction mode.

I mumbled my acknowledgments and absorbed their penetrating stares as they gave me head to toe once-overs and I took the opportunity to do the same.

They both had long, lean faces and long, lean bodies, like greyhounds. Their hair was slicked back, in classic 'matinee idol meets teddy boy' style, with lashings of Brylcreem. They smelt exotic. Even from the other side of the table I was keenly aware of their scent; it was anything but feminine and quite intoxicating. They smiled bored smiles that revealed pointy, nicotine-stained teeth, the only letdown in the otherwise sexy aura that emanated from them as they flashed their glinting green eyes in our direction.

"Hello, Sophia. Nice to meet ya,'" Charles said in a slow cockney drawl that almost made me laugh, but I didn't dare. He sounded like Sid James trying to do bad Hollywood. Evidently, he thought it sounded cool. It wasn't.

He reached out his hand to shake mine and I was aware of the missing little finger and the big, bright, garish, jewel-encrusted gold rings on every other one that he had been able to retain. I caught a flash of a heart-shaped tattoo on his palm, filled with initials, as he pressed it against mine and then it was gone, slipped back into his pocket like the other one as he slouched back into his chair.

We joined them as Eddie poured champagne for both of us.

A first for me.

I sipped.

I liked.

I sipped again.

And again.

Eddie poured more and chit-chatted with Anita as she snuggled up next to him. It was obvious they were well known to each other and their intimacy spoke volumes, although I was only half aware of so many things that night, it being all so new and me being so overawed. I had clearly entered an adults' world and I was out of my depth. I really didn't know how to behave. What was expected of me.

Charles moved closer and tried to get friendly. I was nervous and answered in monosyllables as I stared wide-eyed around the room, taking in a visual feast with eyes the size of dinner plates. It was all too much to absorb at one glance - the well-dressed men, the elegant women, the hostesses, the dim lighting, the elegant furniture and the heady aroma of perfume, cologne and cigarette smoke; lots of cigarette smoke. The champagne meanwhile was rapidly helping to ease my anxiety.

"Sorry, what were you saying?" I turned my face towards Charles and smiled.

"She's the same age as me," said Anita, briskly intercepting the question to avoid any indiscretion on my part. "Twenty-one."

"Pfff! You're not twenty-one!" chimed Eddie. "You can't fool me." He grinned and nodded his head towards me. "And neither is she."

"We both are, and that's an end to it," she snapped, before picking up the champagne glass and guzzling the contents, followed by a loud belch that seemed hilarious to everyone but me.

"Whatever you say, darlin'. You know me – always believe what I'm told." He smirked and Charles sniggered.

I cringed inwardly as I tried to figure out what situation

I had gotten myself into - or more specifically - what Anita had gotten me into. It was all very well for her. She could assert herself in an environment like this. I could sense her revelling in the glamour, the glitz, the naughtiness of it all and her being the centre of a great deal of attention.

I, on the other hand, wanted to shrivel up and curl into a ball.

Charles meanwhile was being very friendly towards me and I was beginning to understand that I had been set up as his date. Anita was obviously Eddie's 'girl' and she thought I would be a nice match for his brother.

"Where are you from then, Sophia?" Eddie asked, leaning over the table and smiling broadly.

"Near Epsom."

"Aaah. Epsom. The stockbroker belt. That why you talk all lardy-dah, is it? Got a good education, did ya'? Just like Anita here." He squeezed her close. "You've 'ad an education alright, ain't ya, sweetheart?"

She forced a smile and nodded. "Go to the Ladies Room, shall we, Sophia? Powder our noses."

She took my hand and, dragging me to my feet, led me to the ladies' room.

"Well, what do you think?"

"Think of what?"

"Well, Charles, of course?"

"I don't know," I said vaguely. "I haven't really given him much thought. Should I?"

"Well, you ought to. He's loaded. So's Eddie. That's why I hang around with him." She gave me a twinkly-eyed grin. "He gives me stuff."

"Stuff?"

"Yes, stuff. You, know - gifts - jewelry - money."

"What for?"

"What for? What d'you think what for?"

I looked at her quizzically.

She stared at me wide-eyed. "Letting him have his way with me."

"You mean …"

She jiggled her head.

"Yes - that," she said answered and blushed a little. "I told him about you and he was really curious to meet you. Asked me to bring you along to meet Charlie-boy." She leaned forward and touched my arm. "But don't ever tell him I called him that. He hates nicknames."

She turned and pulled out her lipstick as a rat-faced girl with buggy, waterlogged eyes slipped into the room with us.

"You OK, love?" Anita asked sympathetically.

"No, I'm not," she yelped and stepped back out of the ladies' room, leaving us alone again.

Anita winced. "Not surprised looking like that. What an ugly cow. She'll never get through the night without being called a few things she won't want to hear. Why would you come to a place like this looking like that?" She rolled her eyes.

She leaned in towards the mirror and carefully re-applied her lipstick and touched up her mascara, cooing admiringly and smiling at herself. She seemed utterly self-absorbed and I honestly hadn't realized that she was so narcissistic - or so cruel.

"You keep saying you want somebody with lots of money to keep you comfortable. Well, now's your chance. Play your cards right and you'll have him eating out of your hand and keeping you in the good life."

"Is that what Eddie does for you?" I asked.

"Not yet," she replied coyly. "But I'm working on it. Come on, let's go back and, remember, work your magic."

"I don't have any."

"Course you do. You just don't realise it."

"Well, I don't know how to work it then."

"So now's your chance to learn." She grabbed my arm and pulled me along behind her. "Just watch me. I'll have them eating out of my hand." She turned her head and winked at me. "I always do."

After we took our seats again at Charles and Eddie's table it became clear that they both only had eyes for me. It didn't take long for Anita to notice this too and take exception to it. As the minutes went by her smile faded, her brow beetled, her hands twitched and her chatty, effusive and engaging attitude slipped away, replaced by a sour-faced, indignant look of barely controlled fury.

Suddenly, she unfolded her arms and grabbed Eddie's arm.

"Eddie, can I have a word with you," she said harshly, yanking him to his feet and dragging him to the other side of the room.

They were still within my range of sight and as Charles blathered on about all the people he knew and how much money he made and how surprised I would be at all the pies he had his gold-encrusted fingers in, I glanced furtively at them arguing at the other side of the large and extremely full room. They were hard to see in all that activity but one thing was very clear. They were both extremely angry, first Anita and then Eddie. There was a great deal of finger pointing going on as both bodies strained towards each other like fighting dogs, barking and snarling.

This did not bode well for a pleasant evening I thought.

"Oi - are you listening to me?" Charles snapped, leaning further over the table and scowling at me. "I'm not paying all this money for fancy champagne and not get anything in return. I could 'ave any woman in this room, you know, so don't think you're so special."

I was shaken.

I wasn't used to being alone and out of my depth with

people I didn't know and couldn't trust. I had thought I could trust Anita and that, together, we could safely make our way into the world of grown-ups. I was quickly realising that I didn't actually know her except that now she was not to be trusted. I was coming to the realisation that the big bad world was something I was simply not prepared for.

'Sorry," I replied, smiling as sweetly as I could.

He grinned, pulled out the seat next to him and indicated for me to join him. I did. He put his arm around my shoulder, which made me tense up and he sensed it.

"What the fuck is the matter with you? You know why you're here, sweetheart. Just like Anita. She knows how to play the game. Didn't she teach you?"

I was about to grab my purse and make my way to the ladies' room again to give me time to think when Anita stormed back to our table in a blind fury and grabbed her bag. She leaned heavily across the table and stared into my face.

"They're all yours, love," she yelled, "if you want them. They seem to want you not me, so go ahead - enjoy yourself. Be my guest, because I'm off."

With that she stormed out of the ballroom and left me sitting there, stunned and fearful. What was I to do? I didn't have the faintest idea of how to deal with the situation, made worse by the fact that, in my state of anxiety, I had been sipping copious amounts of free-flowing champagne. I was starting to feel decidedly not myself.

Suddenly I panicked and made a dash for the door to catch up with Anita. As I reached the vestibule, I saw her receding back slip out and onto the street. I ran after her but she was in a cab and on her way to god knows where before I could reach her.

So here I was - tipsy and breathless - standing on the kerb in the pouring rain as my only connection to this new other world that I had found myself in disappeared into the distance in a black taxi.

And I was getting soaked.

I had no coat, no purse, no money and they wouldn't let me back in.

What a pathetic figure I made.

I started to cry as a blanket of self-pity settled over me.

I had never been so alone or out of my depth. I hadn't a clue what to do next, until my fuzzy head cleared enough for me to remember two things. One was the fact that I had a one pound note hidden inside my bra. Stella had told me over and over to do that and, even though I was almost sick of her repeating it, I was now also truly grateful that she had.

The other thing I remembered was Ronnie's phone number. Of course I remembered my home number too but phoning home was the last thing I wanted to do after Stella's stern words about Anita and the trouble she could get me into. Worse still, I had lied to Stella about where we would be tonight and the last thing I wanted to do was prove myself as someone who she thought she could trust, but couldn't.

It wasn't quite midnight, so some restaurants and cafés were still open. I slipped into one and a sympathetic waitress gave me a towel to wrap around me after I had ordered a coffee and waited for the change that would give me the coins for the payphone.

The waitress could see I was upset and, it being a quiet night, she was more than happy to chat and have her curiosity satisfied. She clucked and tutted and gave me her firm opinion that all men were bastards and that nothing - nothing at all - would ever change that.

'Listen, duck. Why don't you use that phone over there be'ind the counter? Make it quick and I'll make sure he don't charge yer,'' she said, pointing her finger at the bored proprietor, who was looking restless, idling at the back of the café until he could close up and go home.

I gratefully took her up on her offer and, as I dialled the numbers, I prayed that Ronnie would be home. His phone was in the living room and I knew it would take him a while to get out of bed and reach it but he picked up on the second ring.

"Hello," he said warily.

"Oh, thank god you're home." I was about to burst into tears, I was so grateful. And then, abruptly, that's exactly what I did.

"What the hell's the matter? Are you alright?"

"I am now I'm talking to you," I sniffled. "Listen, Ronnie, I feel awful asking you this but can you come and get me? I don't have time to explain right now."

I gave him the address and he was about to ask what the hell I was doing there but I cut him off.

"Please just come and get me."

And, without another word, that's exactly what he did.

As luck would have it, he had the company car at home and so it took him less than twenty minutes to get there at that time of night. The café was closed now but the waitress, Rosie - bless her soft, warm, generous heart - insisted on staying with me until Ronne arrived.

I kept an eagle eye out for the car and, seeing him before he saw us, I waved frantically to catch his attention. I don't think I had ever been happier to see anyone in my life before and, when he was barely out of the car, I hugged him closely to me and started to cry.

"Blimey, Sophe, what's got you in such a state?"

"Man trouble! What else?" Rosie said with a big sigh. "They're never worth it. Oh - and alcohol. It's usually not worth it - ever."

"Sorry? You are?" Ronnie asked as he wrapped me in his raincoat, ready to bundle me in the car.

"Never mind me. I was just keeping an eye on your

friend 'til you got here."

"She's a lifesaver," I said. "Rosie looked after me. Didn't you, Rosie?"

"If you say so, luv," she said with a tired smile. "Anyway, must be off. Take good care of your friend. She's had a right old shake up tonight, I reckon. Cheerio, sweetheart."

She patted my shoulder, turned on her heels and bustled off down the street. Ronnie hustled me into the passenger seat and settled himself in to drive me home.

"What the hell's been going on?"

So I told him and he didn't say a word until I had finished.

"I should have known that Anita would have something to do with it. She's trouble, that one, and no mistake."

"I'm beginning to see that now."

"And what was the place you went to?"

"It was called The Round Table"?

"The Knightsbridge Round Table?"

"Perhaps. Anita just called it The Round Table."

Ronnie whistled softly. "You're well out of it, Sophia. Well out of it. Not the sort of place for you, my girl. That's a hangout for low life and criminals from what I've heard."

"You know it?"

"Heard of it. Let's just say it's not the sort of place for respectable girls to be caught hanging around in. And what were the names of those two blokes? Charles and Eddie?"

I nodded.

"Twins?"

I nodded again.

"Then I think you had a lucky escape," Ronnie said through clenched teeth, staring intently at the slick and sodden road ahead. "I'd bet you any money they're the Peters brothers. Got a bad name for all sorts of reasons. What the hell was someone like Anita doing hanging around with them? She's barely out of school. They'd eat her alive and spit her out without a second thought." He glanced briefly in my direction. "You too, for that matter."

"I've got myself in a bit of a mess, haven't I?" I touched his hand lightly where it lay on the gear shift.

"Nothing like the mess you could have ended up in, thank god."

"Don't tell your mum, will you? I didn't quite tell her the truth about where we were going tonight."

"No doubt," Ronnie exclaimed. "She would have locked you up in the attic and thrown away the key if you had."

"She'll have my guts for garters if she finds out."

I told him about my sleuthing, following Anita home and seeing her disappear into a grim and grimy, miserable terraced house that was anything but the stately home she aspired to.

"It was in a state alright," I said with a grim smirk.

"Maybe we should go round there tomorrow and you can ask her what the hell's going on. Mum's not expecting you home until tomorrow some time, right? So you can stay with me until then."

"What'll I wear? And I don't have any makeup."

Ronnie sighed. "Good grief. I'm sure we'll get around that. Besides, that should be the least of your worries, my girl. You just managed to escape big trouble so I think anything else will be pretty easy to figure out."

We drove in silence the rest of the way and Ronnie bundled me up and into his flat as quickly as he could before tucking me up in his own bed.

"I'll sleep on the sofa." Ronnie said as I was about to protest. "No arguing. The sheets are clean."

I was just glad to be safe and sound again.

"Thank you so much. I don't know what I would have done if you hadn't been home when I called. I've never felt so - I don't know - vulnerable? And scared."

"Well, it was lucky I wasn't out having a good time," he said cheerfully. 'Or out somewhere looking for a good time." He gave me a kiss on the cheek. "Listen. Tomorrow I think you should go and visit your friend Anita and find out what the bloody hell she's up to. Do you remember the address you followed her to?"

"No, but I remember how to get there."

"OK. Tomorrow I'll take you there."

13

Crashed and Burnt

Sophia's story...

THE NEXT DAY, RONNIE WAS TRUE to his word.

I made a slow start and heard him bustling around the flat while I kept the covers over me and tried to forget the mess I had gotten into the night before. A little before eleven, Ronnie tapped on the door to offer me coffee and he sat on the bed as I sipped it slowly and rejoined the world.

"I was thinking about all this and I reckon she's got a screw loose - split personality or something - but she reminds me of Christine Keeler. Do you remember her?"

"Can't say I do."

"No. You were probably too young. She nearly took down the government because she was a naughty girl. Got mixed up with a government minister named Profumo. He got found out having hanky-panky with the young Miss Keeler - very young in fact - and one thing led to another. It was an absolute bloody mess."

"Why does that remind you of Anita?"

"Well, do you really think she's from some fancy family and got all that stuff she's got from the goodness of their big, bloated plutocratic hearts?"

After seeing her steal the jewels so proficiently, I had to admit that I had begun to have grave doubts. Coupled with the discovery of her apparent home in some miserable London backstreet, my doubts were now compelling me to think that things were very far from what she would have us all believe.

"I don't know what to believe any more."

"Christine Keeler mixed with all the big names in town, if you believed everything you read about the 'Profumo affair' as it was called. But the press soon found out that she lived in some miserable little glorified shack with a mother who could barely cope with her and a stepfather who liked her a bit too much, if you get my drift, or so the story goes. So she did what it took to push herself up and out of that and get somewhere in the world. Needless to say, a lot of it wasn't exactly legal or the kind of stuff that gets printed in Tatler." He smiled and patted my hand. "Sound like someone we might know? Oh, and Christine was very attractive too and that's what attractive women do - make the most of their assets. You're not the first one to think of marrying up." He laughed and I grinned sheepishly. "Trouble with Miss Keeler though was that it wasn't so much marriage that she was after but cock. She liked that a lot. Especially a bit of black, apparently. Or more than a bit as the story goes. Couldn't get enough of it. And who can blame her? Who wouldn't?" he said with a smirk. "I'd probably be lined up right behind her for some of that."

"Ronnie! Don't be so dirty. You're making me blush."

"Oh, please! Miss butter-wouldn't-melt-in-her-mouth!" He rolled his eyes. "You know what they say about black dick?

"No, what?"

"Biggest and best in the world apparently. When you've had black cock nothing else will do. I'll have to try it."

I slipped under the covers and shouted repeatedly for him to shut up and go away.

He chuckled. "Anyway, when you're dressed and ready I'll make you some lunch and we'll go on a fishing expedition and see what we can catch. Sound good?"

"Sounds good." I said, muffled under the bedclothes. "Now stop that rude talk and go."

I took my time in the bathroom while Ronnie rummaged through his wardrobe and came up with an old pair of jeans and a white Oxford shirt that turned out to provide quite a respectable outfit once I had turned up the jean cuffs and which, coupled with my black stiletto shoes, proved to be more than suitable for a Sunday afternoon of confrontation with a very pretty, hot-headed and inscrutable young woman. With butterflies dive-bombing my stomach, we drove to the address that I had followed her to that day after class. Ronnie dropped me a couple of doors away.

"No wonder she wanted to do what it took to get herself out of here if this really is where she lives." He said sniffily as he pulled up at the kerb.

"Well, we'll soon find out." I sighed.

"It's just about the worst house in the street too. What a dump!" said Ronnie disdainfully.

"Wish me luck," I said as I got out of the car. "And don't go anywhere."

"I'll be here. I wouldn't leave a car like this unattended on this street even if it was locked."

I walked anxiously to the house that I remembered her slipping into. I would have opened the gate except it had already fallen off its hinges. The front garden - what little of it there was - was full of weeds and bits of rubbish. Looking at it closely for the first time, my heart sank. I knocked tentatively on the door and waited.

I could hear some activity deep inside and a couple of voices shouting. Eventually the door was opened by a sour looking, pimply teenage boy who looked as if he hated everyone.

"Yeah? Can I 'elp you?"

"Is Anita in?"

"Yeah. Who wants 'er?"

"Tell her it's Sophia."

He turned his head and shouted down the dark passage behind him.

"Hey, 'nita, it's someone for you." He turned back to me. "Hang about. She'll be here in a sec."

He left the door ajar and disappeared back into the darkness of the house and I shuffled my feet nervously on the doorstep before Anita stepped up and swung back the door.

"Oh! It's you. What the hell are you doing here?" She looked furious. "How'd you find me?"

"I followed you one day after class."

"Oh you did, did you? Is that something a friend would normally do then?"

"And what about last night? Is that something a friend would normally do? You put me in an awful situation."

"Did I? Seemed to me you was doing just fine with two rich fellas falling all over you to get into your knickers."

In the heat of her emotions her voice had changed from her suave and cultivated home counties tinkle to a common cockney twang. Her mask was slipping and her roots were clearly showing.

"What do you mean?"

"What do you mean?" she repeated in a screeching parody of me. "What do you bloody well think? I take you out on a blind date - as a favour to every bugger except me - and what do you do? You steal 'em both."

"I never intended to."

"Well you did."

"If I'd known where we were going and what you were up to, I would never have gone. Auntie Stella warned me to be careful."

"Well, that nosy old cow can mind her own bloody business from now on. Not that there's likely to be a next time now, I reckon." She hissed as she swept her hand expressively at the street. "This is my country home? D'you like it? Not quite what you had in mind, is it?"

Despite the look of hard anger on her face, I could see that her eyes had moistened and realised that, for her, the game was going horribly wrong. Ronnie and I were dabbling in a light-hearted version of 'My Fair Lady' but, for Anita, this was a high-stakes game as full of risk and danger as any James Bond thriller. She was travelling a much more dangerous road where every day could be her unravelling. I could see that now.

"Why didn't you tell me? Why all the lies?"

She snorted. "I wouldn't know where to start. It's alright for you. You're already on safe ground. Whatever happens to you, you'll be alright." She paused and wiped a tear away. "You were so envious of me, weren't you? Do you know what that feels like? It's like a drug. It's addictive when you get people tied up in your spell and I need it. For now, it's the only weapon I've got."

"Can I come in? We can talk about it."

She looked at me for a long time before answering.

"Nope. I don't think so." She paused before cutting our connection for good. "Have a nice life, Sophia."

She slammed the door in my face and I stood there, momentarily stunned, before trotting quickly back to the car.

"Well?"

"That's her home and everything she's ever said is obviously a lie."

"Blimey, she's a piece of work. Mum was right."

"Yes, but you know the sad thing? She's in a bad way. She's so full of anger she's going to explode one day soon and it won't be pretty. I saw it all over her face."

"She's nothing but trouble, that one. You're better off out of it."

"Yes, but I really feel sorry for her."

"Don't! They make their own beds, then they try and get other people to lie there with them. She won't be the first and she won't be the last. That Christine Keeler was the same. She damaged a lot of lives - destroyed some of them. The chap that discovered her - Stephen Ward - he made her what she was. Took her from nowhere to somewhere special and thanks to her, he ended up killing himself. So keep away. People like that are dangerous. Look what she almost did to you already."

"But don't you think she needs help?"

"I'm sure she does but that's not your responsibility. Only she can do that." Ronnie squeezed my hand. "Come on. Let's get you home. Mum will be wondering what's happened to you and I for one have no intention of telling her the truth."

Ronnie put the car in gear and sped sharply away, putting much needed distance between Anita and me. As we drove out of London he told me the story of Christine Keeler and Stephen Ward. We both thought it ironic how much it resembled what Ronnie and I were doing, only our plans were safe and risk free in comparison.

We put on our best smiles and cheeriest dispositions for Stella and Freddie and there were no questions asked except whether I had a nice time. I lightheartedly lied my way through tea time and, eventually, into bed and the whole episode was forgotten.

Except by me.

Anita had been an extraordinary influence on me. Such determination and enthusiasm. Such self-confidence and willfulness, coupled with looks and personality. It was an outwardly winning combination, unlike any other that I had experienced. And yet it was just a shell because inside lurked a completely different person that I couldn't stop worrying about.

She stopped coming to class - just dropped out of sight - but eventually she did re-surface about a month later. I saw her before she saw me. She was waiting for me at the entrance to the station where we usually split after classes to each make our own way home.

She looked a mess.

Her hair was pulled back in a pony-tail and looked greasy. She had an old anorak on, pulled close about her as she crossed her arms over her chest. Her jeans were old and dirty; her sneakers worn and badly soiled.

She turned and saw me just as I was wondering if I should slip behind something and hide. I was not sure if this meeting would be a good thing because I didn't know what, if any, spell she still had over me, but a spell she clearly had.

Wretched would be the word to use to describe her. I had never seen her look anything other than radiant but this was a different Anita - another person entirely - as she shuffled towards me, barely able to make eye contact.

"What's happened to you?"

"Oh - just about everything," she groaned.

"Look. Let's go to 'The Milky Way' and I'll buy you a coffee."

It was our local coffee bar, where we would frequently pop in on our way home after classes to daydream and fantasize about our futures. In our dreams they would always be full of excitement and promise but, for Anita, apparently not anymore. There was no promise on her horizon as far as I could tell and, as we strolled, she talked.

"I'm sorry for getting you in trouble, Sophia."

"You didn't really. It didn't go that far."

"But it could have." She glanced towards me as we walked on. "Trouble is what I specialise in, Sophia. You're best to be well out of my way."

We reached the café and took a table near the back where it was quiet and we could talk privately with no chance of disturbance, or being seen by other students that we knew. I went to the counter and ordered two milky coffees. They weren't lattes or flat whites in those days, just a good old-fashioned milky coffee. As I went back to join Anita, I saw that she had her head in her hands and looked so lost. I couldn't help feeling that, no matter what the story would be that she would tell me, she was in big, big trouble.

"Are you going to tell me what's wrong?" I whispered and put my hand on hers. Tears welled up in her eyes at my touch.

"Oh, Sophia. I've made such a bloody awful mess of things and I just can't stop myself."

"What's happened?"

"What hasn't, is more like," she sighed and paused. "Sophia, I'm pregnant. My mother's kicked me out of the house because she thinks it's my step-dad's." She scrunched up her face in a look of disgust. "As if I would! He's such a turd. I wouldn't let him so much as shake my hand let alone put his you-know-what you-know-where."

"So where are you staying?"

"Well, I thought Eddie would help me out."

"You mean Eddie as in our bad Saturday night?"

She nodded. "Considering he's the father."

"So what did he do?"

"Told me to get lost, didn't he? Doesn't want to have anything to do with me. Not now I'm in the family way."

"So what are you doing?"

"Staying with a friend. Sleeping on her couch and trying to stop from going under. When I'm up, I'm up. But when I'm down, I'm in the basement. You haven't seen me on a downner before, Sophia and it ain't pretty."

The waitress brought our coffees and we paused for a moment.

"What are you going to do about it?"

"Get rid of it."

"Really?"

"Of course, don't be so fucking naïve, Sophia." she hissed. "There is no way on this earth that I can have this baby because, if I do, it'll be the death of me or the baby or quite possibly both."

"Why?"

"Because I'll kill it, or me," she stared directly into my eyes. "Despite appearances to the contrary, I am a fucking train wreck under the surface."

"So what can I do?"

"Give me money. It's that simple." She sighed. "I don't have it and it seems no-one else does either."

"What makes you think I have it?"

"I don't but you're the only person I can think of who might."

"Well I don't. How much do you need anyway?"

"A couple of hundred."

"Quid?"

"No. Cigarettes," she snapped. "Of course quid, what d'you think?"

"Well I don't have it."

"But you can get it."

"Where from?"

"That doll-faced queer you're always going on about."

"Ronnie?"

She nodded. "Or his parents, who seem to want to give you everything you ask for."

She looked as if a bad smell had passed under her nose.

"You don't have to be so nasty about the people you hope are going to help you," I snapped back and half rose from my chair, ready to walk out.

She put her hand on mine.

"I'm sorry – really sorry. Don't hate me, Sophia. I just can't help it. I've turned into the biggest bitch this side of Watford."

"You always were, Anita," I said.

She looked about to bite my head off until she saw the twinkle in my eye and we both laughed.

"Christ! I can't remember when I laughed last. I'm surprised I didn't crack my face." She looked down at her hands and was quiet for a moment. "I know I'm asking a lot and I know I don't deserve it, but if you can help I'll be in your debt forever."

"I can't promise anything, Anita, because I don't have it and I have to try and get it."

"But you will?"

"Try? Yes, I'll try. How do I get in touch with you?"

"You can't. Can I call you?"

"OK. Call me at my aunt and uncle's. Just say you're a friend called Mary and leave a day and time to meet here again. But give me at least a week."

"OK."

I scribbled the phone number on a spare piece of paper in my bag and she tucked it away in her pocket. We made small talk for a while as we finished our coffees and then left.

"Thanks, Sophia, for trying to help. You've been a good friend and I treated you badly." She hugged me. "I'm sorry for that," she said in a sad, low and weary voice. "I was jealous of you, you see, and I got spiteful - to put it mildly." She laughed derisorily and rolled her eyes.

"I envied you, but why were you jealous of me?"

"Because you have it all - looks, personality and people who care about you and I don't. One way or another you'll do just fine but me? I'm going to have to fight tooth and nail to get myself somewhere safe and comfortable and look where I am now already. In the shit." She sighed. "Just don't give in too easily, Sophia. Don't take the first half-decent bloke that comes along and settle for second best. Your cousin is right. You deserve better than that."

She turned and went her way. I watched her go and had the feeling that I would never see her again.

Then I turned and went mine.

Anita did call and left a message to meet her and I made my way to 'The Milky Way' at the set time and on the set day but she never showed up. I was dreading it because I didn't have the money. Didn't even have the wherewithal to ask for it. I would have to lie to Stella and I just couldn't do that. It would have to be the truth or not at all and I knew she would want no part of it.

Ronnie too. I assumed, rightly or wrongly, that he would want to wash his hands of it so the question never got asked and I didn't know how I was going to tell Anita without her screaming obscenities at me. So, when she didn't show up, I thanked my lucky stars and, after waiting half an hour, I skedaddled out of there and didn't look back.

She never phoned again and disappeared out of my life.

Then the news started to circulate and, several months after I saw her disappear down the street for the last time, one of my classmates asked me had I heard the news.

What news?

About Anita.

I braced myself.

There were conflicting stories but the one constant theme was that she had been killed in a car crash. The driver was as drunk as she was and, as so often happens, drink and driving didn't mix well that night.

The funeral was long gone by the time I knew this so I didn't get a chance to say goodbye. I could have visited her family I suppose to find out more but thought better of it.

But she lived on in my head.

She had been a conundrum. A puzzle I hadn't solved and now never would. She was also a wake-up call. Unintentionally, she had alerted me to danger, shaken off some of my naïveté and taught me not to be so trusting. I often wondered just how thick that hard shell was that she flaunted so boldly. Wafer thin perhaps. Just one crack and she was exposed and vulnerable.

As the years went by, I often wondered if she had been bipolar. But what the hell was that in the sixties? No-one knew about such things then as she soared as high as a kite, feeling the intensity of life like a tire feels the road. Everything was amazing to her and people were drawn to her dynamism, energy and magnetism like a moth to a flame, me included. She was convinced of her desirability and thrived on the admiration and flattery of others as if it was mother's milk. If I didn't see that then, I see it now.

I think it was despair and pain that took her down, a longing to be out of it all, and the car was just the chosen weapon. In the end, I don't think she had the energy she needed for life.

I would never know now.

"Don't take the first half-decent bloke that comes along and settle for second best." She had said. "You deserve better than that."

Her words stuck with me.

14

Equal Rights

Sophia's story...

THROUGHOUT ALL OF THIS, ELLEN, PETER and Ronnie remained my close friends and mentors. I visited Ronnie's flat more often and we would all congregate and drink wine and chat late into the night as they helped to plan my education in the facts of life.

First I was to meet a whole new breed - the lesbians.

As agreed, I went to one of Ellen's *LOVE* meetings, being held in a hall above a pub in Battersea. Ellen had given me detailed instructions how to get there. It was easy enough on the train and a short walk to the pub on Battersea Park Road. In 1965, Diana Vreeland, Editor of 'Vogue' magazine, declared London 'the most swinging city in the world' but, from where I was looking, it didn't appear to have even had a push yet, let alone be swinging.

It was all a bit rough and down at heel, the buildings all soot-soaked. Even the people looked as worn out and drab as the streets themselves and, as I reached the pub, already lively with people shrugging off the shabbiness of their neighbourhood, I wondered if this was the best place for a women's meeting, especially *those* sorts of women. To make matters worse, we all had to walk through the pub to get to the room upstairs, hired for the event.

Once I had found out where to go, I pushed my way through the crowd as quickly as I could and joined the rest of the women upstairs, all looking rather uncomfortable and brittle as if their knickers were made of steel wool. Impending disaster was in the air and many looked as if they could smell it, being used to impending disaster as many of them were.

Ellen was there, looking as radiant and fiery as a pixie could and, despite her boyish looks, she was the most feminine and attractive woman there. I had the dubious distinction of being the only other 'looker' in the bunch.

There was a small table at the front with three chairs lined up behind it and Ellen took the middle chair, flanked by two sour-looking, middle-aged women. One was big and buxom, the other pale and emaciated. If the table had been a boat it would have instantly capsized to starboard.

Ellen made the introductions. The other women were to give talks. One, on the matter of equal pay, was given by the plump one, who was clearly already enjoying the economics of such a scenario and the other, on the matter of household violence, was given by the thin woman, who looked as if she had just escape the worst of it by the skin of her teeth.

All in all, the gods did not seem to be shining down on this event and the visiting drunks from downstairs seemed to agree as they started to gather at the back of the room after visiting the 'Gents' toilets, distractedly doing up their flies and adjusting their tackle.

All was in precarious harmony until one of the men, lively from one too many beers, asked if any of the women would like to adjust his tackle for him, just as the skinny woman was providing enlightening information about spousal rape. At that point, needless to say, the men were all ears and cheering in firm support of such a thing.

The man who requested that his tackle be adjusted decided that there weren't any women there who he would want to adjust his tackle, and he made that opinion firmly known to everyone. None, that is, except the kid at the front table.

That would be Ellen.

And the pretty one with the nice tits.

That was me.

I knew, because he was pointing clearly at me.

This was all quite funny in hindsight except that I was the wrong person to be the subject of a drunken man's lewd approaches. I had been there before and was still recovering from it, still weak at the knees from the last fall.

This, I knew, wouldn't do me much good.

Then, suddenly, through the sounds of male guffaws and the occasional whimpering of women, Ellen strode across the room and confronted the men.

"You lot can just fuck off, do you hear me? Fuck off! Go on, fuck off! You've no right to be here and we don't want you here. Got it?"

The men all seemed to think it was very amusing. The women, naturally, didn't and Ellen refused to let up on the swearing until they started to move out. Someone muttered "Well, she's got some spunk in her that one. Fair do."

"Yeah, and she can 'ave some more an' all," came the cry from a tall, stocky man in overalls, standing at the front of the crowd, leering as he put both hands behind his back and shoved out his pelvis provocatively in a gesture that even the most prudish virgin in the room couldn't fail to interpret.

His large bulge was there for all to see and, were it not for the strong principles that brought these women here, I suspect a few of them might have wanted to have a go.

Someone had obviously slipped downstairs and called the licensee because a burly man with an apron and a rolling pin, who I'm sure was not a cook, arrived. With a lot of shouting and waving of hands he got the lads out and closed off the room.

"Take this key and lock it from the inside until all this cools down, OK?" He said to Ellen. "Nice language by the way. I admire a woman who knows how to swear and doesn't mind doing it," he added with a wink.

And there we were, locked inside. Safe and sound against the men, which seemed appropriate considering the event.

We were all a bit stunned and many were visibly upset. It was all a bit of a joke to the lads but did untold damage to some of the women there, and some of that damage would be to me. I could feel it through my still quickened pulse.

"Well, that was a fucking disaster!" It was Ellen, still fuming. "I can't fucking believe that stupid woman booking a place like this. She should have come to see it first. Honestly, I could murder her."

"Who?"

"Susan - the fat, ugly cow over there with the flat face. Sorry. I shouldn't talk like that but, really, she's always screwing up." Ellen paused and heaved a big, big sigh before taking my hands and staring at me. "This sort of thing never happens and it would happen on your first time, wouldn't it? I'm really, really sorry."

"It's OK. I did learn something tonight though."

"You did? I'm glad. What was that?"

'That I'm clearly far from healed' is what I thought to myself. What I said was "I've got a lot to learn about women's issues."

And I did learn. I went to a few *LOVE* meetings and began to understand why women were taking up the cudgel against all the unfairness that I never realised existed. I had never thought about it before, not *really* thought about it. I was rediscovering the three "W's", just as I did as a child - the why's, the where's and the when's of everything that women needed to fight against.

I had always thought of myself as the only damaged teenage girl, and my mother the only woman whose life had been made wretched by a good-for-nothing husband.

But the world, it seemed, was full of them.

One of each was unfortunate.

A world full of them was disgraceful and, through it, I learnt indignation.

Anger I already owned.

But I couldn't keep up with Ellen. She was committed right to the top of her pretty, little head whereas I was only enthusiastic enough to get my hands dirty now and again. I gave her moral support where I could but she continued to lead the charge with ever-increasing fervor.

I, on the other hand, was just a follower who happened to be born into increasingly emancipated times which, if I held on tight, would take me where I needed to go. Much as I wished for the same fire in my belly, I had no great ambitions beyond making myself comfortable in life which I would, no doubt, achieve on the backs of raging, angry people like Ellen.

"All those women who are standing up and pushing for change – Germaine Greer, Betty Friedan, your precious Gurley-girl. They're getting me all fired up, Sophia," she would say before her next meeting, and her next, and her next, as the crowds got bigger.

I had to admire her.

15

It's Party Time

Sophia's story...

IN NO TIME MY NINETEENTH BIRTHDAY had arrived and a party was arranged, to be held at Ronnie's flat. After all the time spent with Ellen and her friends over the past couple of years, she had become my closest ally. I knew her motives were not entirely pure. She lusted after me, I could tell, but had the decency not to make any advances, knowing full well that I would not know how to deal with them, or want to.

It seemed to me that she took greater pleasure in admiring me from afar than she would have by bedding me and ruining any hope for friendship, let alone a relationship. One day she amused me by saying in a loud, high voice 'Darling, there are some pussies in this world that you should just never stroke' and looked me straight in the eye.

I have laughed over that many times since.

She and her mixed bag of friends became my new world, and they were invited to join the party, alongside the few new friends that I had made at college.

Ronnie's lie that my parents were dead, first elicited during our Soho dinner, was firmly adhered to. "Your family history deserves to remain exactly that," he said. "History is what it is and we're starting you a new life, so let's give it a fresh new start, shall we? You can keep your parents but, for the rest of the world, they should be what works best for you. Dead and generating sympathy is a good way to go, don't you think?"

He was right. They were dead to me and that's all I had to remember. No-one liked to pry and so I never needed to give any details. I was an orphan and didn't like to talk about it. Simple as that.

By now, Ellen had firmly settled herself into Ronnie's flat, as his flatmate, but they both dropped hints that it was more than that, which made for great gossip and distraction from the reality of their relationship. Back then, false trails led to safety nets if you didn't want to get found out, shamed, and humiliated. London was one of the best and safest places in the world to be queer, but that only went so far. People like Charles, the hair stylist, actually used it to advantage, to give his salon a unique atmosphere, but they were few and far between. Everyone else, conventional people in conventional jobs and living conventional lives, stepped gently and warily, always on the lookout for a false move that could plunge them into the abyss.

To be unmarried after a 'certain age' automatically raised red flags so, consequently, many people struggled against their nature in order to lead those conventional lives that put a lid on their sexual urges until they slowly withered and died or exploded into chaos. When I look back at it now, I can hardly believe the amount of change that has taken place, yet it is still not enough.

Meanwhile, the world ricocheted from one convulsive evolutionary change to another. The sexual revolution was in full force and free love was encouraged for all of us by

American liberals everywhere, but especially by Californians. Youthful experimentation was in full swing with the summer of 1967 designated the 'Summer of Love'.

Drugs were becoming more and more common and the drug culture, for the first time, crept out from under its stone, only to be stamped on wherever possible by the powers that be. Timothy Leary, the famous American writer and psychologist, was arrested for possessing marijuana, and LSD was banned.

Even pop songs were influenced by hallucinogens as The Beach Boys released 'Good Vibrations', The Byrds released 'Eight Miles High' and the Rolling Stones released 'Paint it Black', all of them bringing the exploding drug culture vicariously into everyone's living room, without the risk of side-effects.

We amused ourselves by thinking how much of a kick Norma must be getting with all this enthusiastic love-making going on around her, and how much was she participating? Or was she nicely settled into faithful monogamy with her accountant?

And, of course, the Vietnam War raged on.

For now though, we were enjoying life and Ronnie was fascinated by my life change and living it vicariously while all the world events became just a hazy, distant backdrop to our daily lives. He was having such a great time being, in his words, my 'fairy godmother' as he helped me - his 'Cinderella' - make this great transformation. Accompanying me to salons, where he always had an opinion on the latest look that I should be indulging in, he was determined to create the perfect woman that he himself would love to be.

And, yes, the party was interesting.

To say the least.

Ellen, Ronnie and Peter between them had worked hard to rustle up a group of about twenty eclectic friends and acquaintances, many of whom didn't actually know me but were happy to meet me and, more importantly, enjoy a free party. We all worked hard to impress the guests and they had a ball. I thought of Anita and the fun she would have had commanding everyone's attention, much to Ellen's chagrin.

As Ronnie reminded me over and over again, "This is your coming out, Sophia. Your dry run for entering society. Tonight you'll discover how confident you can be and how you can hold a conversation, and your drink. It's easy to say you can do it, but much harder to actually do it."

My cleavage was a big hit amongst the hot-blooded males and ensured that I had plenty of admirers and lots of attention all night. It was exhausting but I pushed through. Most people were surprised that I had a brain in my head and that I could use it, as we waded through lively conversations about the changing times and the current events. The Profumo Affair, and the subsequent scandal that engulfed all its characters, became the subject for much discussion. There was much heated debate about what befell poor Stephen Ward, as well as Christine Keeler and Mandy Rice Davies. Having known Anita, I proved to be quite liberal - and opinionated - in my support of self-driven young women who crossed the line for reasons that, at least for them, were important and justified.

The food was to be 'continental', so there were dishes of lasagne and beef stroganoff accompanied by plates of garlic bread and, in the land of bland, everyone thought it was highly original. Cheap red wine flowed. People lounged everywhere and laughter echoed throughout the flat.

Unbeknownst to me, my special guest and extra-special gift was an attractive, but fairly unassuming, man by the name of Anthony Rogers. Probably in his early thirties, he was of average height and build, slim but not thin, with thick auburn hair and brown eyes. His skin was classically

English, pale and unblemished, and he was blessed with good teeth, always a rare and treasured commodity.

He was charming and polite, friendly and softly spoken and I was smitten, along with most of the girls at the party, as well as some of the men. He had a certain something that was almost impossible to define that disarmed and charmed almost everyone, men and women alike.

"Anthony is another present of mine," whispered Ronnie, smiling. "But there's a story to him that I need to share with you first before you even think of unwrapping that gift."

"He's actually my gift too." Ellen sidled up to us as we chatted in the corner. "He's my discovery and I passed him on to Ronnie so that he could think about how useful he might be to you. But, Ronnie, you're going to have to tell her the whole story. My real gift is this," she said, handing me a brightly wrapped package. "Sophia, darling, have you ever actually seen a penis? Do you know what one looks like? Well, this will help. It's an illustrated copy of 'The Kama Sutra' and shows you every position you will ever need to know for sex."

Having unwrapped the gift, she opened it for me. "See that there? That's the penis and at the end is what they call the helmet. Within the helmet lives the head of the penis and within the head of the penis lives a very small brain, the sole purpose of which is to completely destroy the logical workings of the big brain in the man's head. It's very effective and has ruined many a happy marriage, and life for that matter."

"It looks rather harmless," I said naively, and Ronnie and Ellen laughed. "But I presume by your reaction that it's not."

"No, honey, it most certainly is not harmless. In fact, it's quite deadly and has wreaked havoc the world over, probably since man started roaming the earth. It also happens to generate a great deal of pleasure and that's the problem. It's important that you take control of a man's brain but you'll need to control both of them if you want to succeed. And you, darling, are going to do just fine if you keep looking like you do. You have all the men at your mercy tonight, especially the ones whose little brains want you and not Ronnie. Use that power wisely."

"Do you think I have a chance with some of these then?" said Ronnie, somewhat surprised.

"Ronnie, dear. This is Ellen. Do you think I wouldn't have included a few from your team? Well, our team, really. And Peter too, for that matter. I'm sure he's included a few from his group of merry men. Can't you tell? I wouldn't have thought they would be particularly discreet, at least not in friendly territory like this."

"Well, I'm not doing a very good job of picking up the signals then." Ronnie smiled.

"Work harder!" said Ellen before turning again to me. "You need to spend some time reading this book. It'll open up another world to you. Ronnie and I both think that the next step in your education is to become sexually aware, darling. It's all the rage," she exclaimed. "And it's so enjoyable once you get the hang of it. And you really *do* need to get the hang of it."

I rifled through the first few pages and asked, with a rather quizzical look, "Are there this many ways to - you know - do it?" They both laughed.

"No, dear, there are more," Ellen replied as she took my hand and gave me a look that seemed to indicate she was dealing with a simpleton. "Now, just to make this even more fun, I have also included a photographic copy of the book. The photo one is foreign so you won't be able to read the text but the photos show you what people really do. It's very naughty and quite a turn on! You might get to have some fun of your own with that one. You know, in the privacy of your own bedroom. The other one, as you can see, is much prettier. All those lovely drawings and paintings! And it's in English so that you can understand what they're doing. Between the two of them you'll have some lovely winter evenings alone in bed, with a nice cup of 'Ovaltine' afterwards, as you think about practising the real thing."

I made a mental note to ask Ronnie what I was supposed to 'do' alone in my bedroom with these books as he and I rifled through the pages, intrigued. "Do they have one for people like me?" Ronnie asked, "and, if so, how do I get one?"

"Can't help you there, but I'm sure Sophia will lend you hers and you can use your own imagination to fill in the blanks. Then one more book here is "Sex and the Single Girl" by your heroine Helen Gurley Brown. You don't have a copy already, do you? You'll definitely want to read this a few more times if you plan to become the emancipated woman you seem determined to be. So I thought you should have your own copy instead of having to look in the library all the time." Ellen winked and offered the gift to me with both hands and a small bow. "In honour of your amazing progress, darling."

"All that reading will set you up for next year's project," said Ronnie and winked. "We'll have it all mapped out for you."

I tucked my books in a drawer in Ronnie's bedroom and returned to the party. The lights were dimmed and everyone glowed. I still found it hard to believe how I had changed, like an insect emerging from its chrysalis, one day a maggot, next day a butterfly, in all its splendour.

Thanks to Ronnie and Ellen, my unfocused dreams for my future were rapidly achieving clarity, as I confronted the challenges facing me and overcame them. I wouldn't let Anita down and settle for second best. I promised myself that - and her - so I had to make sure that the next part of my transformation was as carefully handled as the first. No infatuations, no reckless affairs and, most of all, no babies. If I was going to end up where I planned, I needed no diversions.

Anthony caught my elbow and moved in to join me. "Hello again. How is the birthday girl enjoying her party?"

"Absolutely lovely! I was just circling around and thinking how much my life has changed in such a short time."

"Yes. Ronnie was telling me how your parents had both died and that you are living with his family now. It must have been an awful shock, but seems to have worked out well in the end. Ronnie showed me your photo from two years ago. I think he uses that like his badge of honour! He's so proud of you and wants everybody to know what a great job he's done - which he has. I'm not knocking it. You've become the replacement sister for the one he lost to America, I think."

"He's so proud of *himself*, you mean" I said with a smirk. "And his creation. He thinks Dr. Frankenstein created 'Barbie' and that's who we are." Anthony laughed. "And you're right. I think he misses Norma a lot more than he says he does, so made me the substitute. Don't get me wrong. I mean it in the nicest possible way. I take it as a compliment."

"Yes, you should. I've known Ronnie for a few years now. He's not cut from the same cloth as most of us, as you know, but he's got his head screwed on right. Same goes for Ellen for that matter. They are different-sex versions of the same person, I reckon."

"So, Anthony, what is it that you do?" I asked.

"I'm a doctor. I spend my time looking at the ugly side of life. All the aches and pains and the nasty bits of bodies and aging flesh! Don't get me wrong - I love it. But you've got to love it to do it. Dealing with unhealthy people all the time can be a bit soul destroying."

"So what do you do to brighten up your life outside of the surgery?" I asked innocently.

"I'm a gigolo."

"A what?"

"A gigolo. Let's just say I make myself available to women. Usually for free but, sometimes, if they don't really do it for me but I do it for them, they pay me. Gifts, influence or both mostly, but not usually money. That's a bit tasteless, don't you think? It can be quite beneficial when you mix in my circles. You know - titles and money, power and influence. That sort of thing"

I think I must have looked a bit stunned because Anthony smiled ruefully and asked if I wanted to sit down. "No." I said. "I've just never met a - what is it? Gigolo? - before, but it doesn't sound much like work."

We both laughed.

"It's not work, Sophia. It's all pleasure. I just love sex. I can't get enough of it and now, with all that practice, I'm really rather good at it." Anthony smiled and winked.

"So really that's like healing the mind and body as well, isn't it? I suppose that's a lot like doctoring too?" I asked.

"Yes, I suppose you're right. Except I deal with much nicer bodies when I'm doing my night job. I suppose that's my compensation. My yin in exchange for the yang."

"Your what?" I asked

"Yin and yang. It's like opposites that work together to complete the whole. It's Chinese. They have some pretty clever ideas, the Chinese, if you ignore the crazy red revolution that's going on over there right now. Talk about madness on a grand scale."

Ellen sidled over. "You two are very chatty."

"He's telling me what he does for a hobby," I said straight-faced and stared directly at Ellen.

"Oh, I see," she said and we both burst out laughing.

Anthony smiled.

"Sophia had never heard of it," he smirked.

"That's because not many people pursue it as vigorously as you, Anthony," she said, as loudly as she could without drawing too much attention to ourselves.

Ellen leaned in to whisper in my ear. "I hear he's very good. Those books I gave you will show you a lot of what Anthony does in his spare time to make women happy. You can study them and fantasize about him." She turned and grinned at Anthony. "I'm being very flattering, Anthony. It's all good."

"Glad to hear it. Well, ladies, I'll leave you to gossip about me in private. In the meantime, I shall go and inspect the goods - and the bads. See you around."

"He is so yummy, Ellen." I had to admit it. There was no getting around it. He was completely qualified for what he did, or at least for getting women into bed. I could only assume that he lived up to his reputation once he got them there. "He's so cute you just want to mother him, don't you?"

"That's his secret weapon. Well, that's in addition to his other secret weapon, which I'm told will take your breath away and, before you ask, read the books first." Ellen cried. "Yes, I may not be a typical "girly girl" but even I can see where the attraction lies. I think if I was a nice, normal girl with some naughty, normal urges I would be standing in line. He's very particular though. If they're not pretty then they have to have other great attributes, like influence, prestige and money. After all, he's only in it, shall we say, for what he can get out of it. Remember - sex is power. He's certainly not wife hunting."

I was amused and intrigued. My enthusiasm for reading Ellen's gifts becoming a real determination. I mingled some more before the guests started to disperse. Anthony, I noticed, left with a strikingly tall and leggy, long-haired blonde who bore a close resemblance to the actress and future 'Bond girl', Britt Ekland. She was the epitome of sixties sex appeal, and I was sure she would be yet another conquest, but for how long?

When the flat was empty of guests, at around 1 a.m., I joined Ronnie, Ellen and Peter in the living room and flopped down on the couch next to Peter. We all lit up and swigged on our glasses of cheap red wine.

"Does anyone want to smoke a joint?" asked Peter and we all looked at him as if he had asked if he should murder his mother. "What?" He stretched the word for emphasis. "Everybody's doing it these days! Don't you even want to try it? Have any of you ever tried it? I hope you're going to say no, Sophia."

It turned out that, despite the feigned looks of shock, both Ronnie and Ellen were faking it because they had tried it, but 'only occasionally', they wanted to make very clear. They most certainly did not make a habit of it - so they said.

"I'm not asking you to," said Peter. "I just want to know if you want to smoke one, so get off your high horses and join in."

So we did.

I was a bit nervous and Ronnie made sure that I only had a few puffs. The rest of them, meanwhile, shared the whole fat, juicy toke and mellowed even more.

"I can see why this stuff is starting to take the world by storm," said Ellen, stifling a few choking coughs from the harsh smoke and sliding down in her chair.

"Well, Sophe, how was that?" asked Ronnie. "Did you enjoy yourself? You were a big hit. The tits especially were very big hits. More than enough to excite the hot-blooded males, and even the merely warm-blooded ones. Even the poofter boys were admiring them, but probably not for the same reason.

"That's because they wanted some of their own, just like yours." Ellen smirked. "I know I would."

"Ellen tells me that you were fully introduced to Anthony and were suitably impressed."

"Yes. I thought he was lovely," I had to admit.

"See," said Ellen. "It's working. His charm is magnetic. He liked you too, Sophia. In fact, he liked you very, very much. But she wasn't fully introduced to him, Ronnie. If she had been, she'd be lying on her back with her legs open and Anthony doing a gynecological examination with his tongue and her screaming the house down in ecstasy."

"Ellen, could you be a little more graphic?" said Peter. "I don't think we're quite getting the picture."

"Sorry, did I go too far?"

"No further than usual," Peter replied. "Which is always too far"

"It's OK. It's part of your endearing charm, Ellen. That's why we love you. Anyway, Peter, that's a bit like the pot calling the kettle black, don't you think?"

"So, should I be pleased or afraid?" I said warily.

"Oh, don't worry about Anthony. We know him well enough and he knows us, so he wouldn't tamper with you unless he had our blessing, which he would, of course. Just not yet. Anyway, you're going to want to spread your legs and fly away one day soon, and I couldn't think of anyone better than him to get you started."

"I think you mean spread your wings," Peter snickered.

"Peter, darling, I may be drunk and getting high as a kite, but I know exactly what I mean," replied Ellen pointedly, before turning her gaze back to me. "You have to do your homework first, darling. Read the books and then it's time for your practical exam. But it'll be like no exam you've ever had before. Getting an A is going to be much more fun than getting a C or E, I can tell you that right now. You will most definitely be wanting to do your homework."

"I bet he smokes cannabis," said Peter, sucking in the last few breaths of the joint and giggling. "Not to mention access to all kinds of other drugs," he added, ending in a coughing jag.

It was late by now - almost two in the morning - but we decided to empty the few unfinished bottles of wine. Slumping into our seats, wine glasses in hand, we drowsily guzzled the dregs.

"So, how are we going to do this?" said Ellen. "If this was a normal household, Sophia, you would sleep with me to keep you safe from the boys but the boys are quite safe, as it turns out. I, on the other hand, am not and, anyway, my brother probably wants me to himself. So, Sophia, you are probably safest to sleep with your cousin. How weird are we?" Ellen exclaimed. "And besides, you need to be kept safe from predators until you know how to beat them at their own game. So you make sure you read those books I gave you."

"Drink up, boys and girls, the party's over and we all need our beauty sleep," exclaimed Peter, chugging the last few mouthfuls of cheap Bulgarian plonk.

The message was slowly getting through to me. I was their cause and Anthony was their no longer secret weapon. Inwardly, I was thrilled - and terrified - at the prospect and needed to study the books that Ellen had given me.

And study them I did.

My appetite for sex was weak at best, having been fed a foul and bitter brew of indigestible interference for so long. I wavered between feelings of excited anticipation and blind fear.

But I knew I would have to fix it.

That my life might depend on it.

That Anthony was the perfect repairman.

What I didn't know was just how much of my life Anthony would end up fixing.

16

Love Is?

Sophia's story...

More than fifteen years of bickering, contempt, anger, hostility and brutal aggression were the foundations of what I understood to be the relationship between men and women. I had seen lust and desire, disguised as love, in my own family and saw it for what it was.

A hallucination.

I saw, firsthand, what havoc 'love' had caused, and I had seen it everywhere I turned as I grew up in the flats where love was confused with a good shag after a night on the razzle. It made me sick to think about it.

That's not love.

Love, as I was discovering, is companionship, sharing, caring, respect. It's a long, straight road taken at a steady speed, not being thrown around on violent switchbacks that could hurl you from your seat and kill you on impact.

That was the road my mother took.

I wanted the other road. The road to survival and I wanted that to be a safe one. I wanted affection, sharing and caring. I didn't need the adrenaline shot of white-hot lust that would only fade and fizzle in double quick time and leave me with … with what? What my parents had? I had learnt where that would take me and it was a road I never want to travel.

"Ronnie. I just wanted to say thanks for organizing the party last night," I said as we sat, late in the morning, over our first cup of coffee. We were both hungover and Ellen and Peter were still asleep. "I was thinking about everything you've done for me since your parents took me in. I know it's not just you. Your mum and dad have been fantastic. Even Norma. But you've really been a rock. I couldn't have done any of this without you."

Ronnie nodded an acknowledgment and moved to the kitchen to put on a fresh pot of coffee; I followed. We stood at the window looking out over the leafy street, warm and glowing in the late morning sun. People were strolling. Families were out in their gardens. It was all very cozy and comfortable.

"So, what's your next step?" asked Ronnie. "Now that you've proved what you're capable of, you'll need to get a job now and earn your keep. I know mum and dad are really happy to have you stay with them. Mum especially loves to have someone to mother - smother more like! But I think you're ready for other things. One thing that's clear is that you're definitely older than your age. Very mature - head screwed on right, as they say. So I think you can be trusted to do the right thing." He gave me a sideways conspiratorial glance. "So I have a plan …"

"Another plan? Will I like it?"

"Of course you will. You know me. Have I ever let you down? And, besides, it's all just one part of my great master plan for you. You are my big project and this is just the next step."

The fresh pot of coffee was ready and, looking out of the window again, Ronnie suggested, "Let's take our coffee mugs and go for a walk on the common. It's too nice to stay in here and, besides, after last night the fresh air will do us good. Blow these cobwebs away and any remains of our hangovers. Shall we?"

We filled our mugs and made our way to the park, where we settled under a tall oak tree and enjoyed the views across the Common and all the activity as people strolled, played, flew kites, walked dogs.

"This is what I think you should do. Now that you have your diploma why don't you come and work for the agency? We always need shorthand typists and secretaries. Probably not a good idea to come and work in my office, but I can probably get you in another one close by. They'll take you if I recommend you."

"I don't know. I love the idea but it seems almost too good to be true," I said between sips. "Will I be good enough?"

"Oh-oh! Watch out! Here comes the inferiority complex again! Of course you'll be good enough, and that's what you have to say to yourself - every time." He pulled me close. "Every time. Remember that. Oh, and one more thing, Ellen is going to be leaving the flat. She's moving closer to her job in town. One of her girlfriends has a room she can rent. So, if you want, you can move in with me and take her room. With a job of your own you can pay the rent and I can keep you under my wing. Mum would be OK with that. She would love to see us living together so that she could tap you for information on me and tap me for you. So she can make sure that neither of us is stepping out of line. You know mums!" Ronnie gave me a sideways look and put his arm around me for a gentle hug. "So, what d'you think? Sounds like a plan?"

"Yes. It definitely sounds like a plan. Honestly, Ronnie,

I love the idea but I'm scared to death. What if I let you down?"

Ronnie raised his mug to mine and chinked. "You won't. Anyway, it's *you* that you need to be thinking about, not me. Right now I know you better than you know yourself. But that'll change. You'll get more confidence soon, you'll see. You're still learning to live in your shiny, new skin."

We rose from our shady spot and strolled, arm in arm, through the park. Everyone, it seemed, was happy that day, and not just me. People smiled and said hello. Children waved. Dogs bobbed and bounced around us, wagging their tails.

I was on cloud nine.

Ronnie too seemed to be savouring the plan and walked with a half-smile on his face, as did I. We were contagious, I think. Ronnie, I noticed, seemed to gain extra confidence from having me with him. He was more outgoing, staring at people with a warm and friendly face, welcoming cheerful interaction without risk of unexpected retaliation.

"Are you being naughty?" I asked as we passed a couple of middle-aged men who only had eyes for Ronnie.

"Yes. I am being a bit naughty if I have to be honest. I may be good for you but you're also good for me. I'm using you, Sophe." Ronnie exclaimed. "But in the nicest possible way."

What do you mean?" I asked.

Well, us boys have to be a bit careful. We can't help our eyes wandering. It's what we do. Because you never know who you might snag. But you might also give the eye to someone who doesn't appreciate it. With you on my arm they won't think I'm flirting with them, just being friendly, and so no risk of getting a black eye."

"So have you seen anyone to play with?"

"Oh, loads!" Ronnie cried and rolled his eyes. "But then

you wouldn't recognize the signs, would you?" Ronnie stopped and led me to a bench where we sat and discreetly eyed the passers-by.

It proved to be a fascinating interlude.

"First, you look out for the men walking alone or men in two's or three's. That's a good indicator. Take him over there, leaning against the tree. He's keeping an eye on the boys. See how he follows the good-looking ones with his eyes, even after they've passed. He's checking them out to see if they look back. Or, if they're with a woman, he's just admiring them but not expecting anything.

And that one over there, on the bench, he's doing the same thing. He's hoping to get lucky. It's all lots of fun, but you have to be careful. The police like to play this game too. Come on to you and get you in the bushes and then arrest you for indecent behaviour. Get your name in the papers, lose your job, lose your family. It's all pretty pathetic, Sophe. And tragic."

"The police do things like that?"

"All the time! Christ, it really pisses me off when I think about it. Why can't we just be left to live our lives the way we are? It's not as though we're doing any harm to anyone. It's the secrets and lies that do all the damage. I've known men kill themselves after being found out, but it's our nature. It's what we do. What we have to do. As Ellen said at your party, that little head at the end of a cock wields an awful lot of power. It can cause havoc."

Ronnie suddenly looked pensive. It was a glimpse of the other side of him, the one that he shielded constantly with a smile and a cheery façade. Which was the real Ronald? At times like this, it was hard to tell.

"I'm sorry, Ronnie. I don't know anything about these things but I do want to understand. I want you to always be able to talk to me about it."

"Thanks, Sophia. I appreciate it. I really do. I think we're going to end up being each other's best friend. Confidantes. It's great having someone around that you can talk to and that knows everything without being judgemental. Mum's great, but I can't talk about this stuff with her, other than the bare minimum. You and I should grow old together. Keep each other company."

Ronnie pointed discreetly towards the lone man on the bench, who was no longer alone.

"Looks like our friend has got some company."

We both watched the scene unfold. The seated man was probably in his thirties. He was well-dressed in a casual way in tweed trousers, despite the warmth of the day, and an open-neck white shirt. He carried a Sunday newspaper as a diversion from his real purpose. Handsome with short, well-groomed hair and glasses, he appeared every bit the smart and studious professional. Beside him, yet some distance apart, sat a younger man dressed in jeans and a white T-shirt and looking more like James Dean than James Dean ever did, complete with cigarette behind the left ear.

They started to chat.

"This looks interesting. Watch this, Sophia. This is going to be an education for you. I'll bet you ten quid that they are going to get up and walk away together in less than ten minutes. And quite likely into the bushes over there." Ronnie pointed to a large and thick copse of trees behind their bench. "And do you want to know why? So that they can have sex together in the undergrowth where nobody can see them."

"Are you serious?" I sounded shocked. I was.

"Absolutely serious. If they don't have a private place to go to, then they don't have much choice. Sometimes, they just can't wait to get their hands on each other and, sometimes, they like the sense of danger. Don't ask me why, but some people get a kick out of flirting with getting caught. I suppose it depends on how much you have to lose. Not for me. I like some comfort and a bit of lovey-dovey. But then I have my own place to go to, so it's easy. OK. There they go."

Ronnie was right. They wandered off, not quite together. The James Dean type went first and disappeared amongst the trees, followed a little later by the older man, who looked furtively around him.

"Happens all the time around here. It's quite the haunt. Not that most people would ever know unless they had any interest in it. It's all quite discreet. There are lots of different hangouts around town, including the Gents toilets; what they call cottages. Isn't that quaint?" Ronnie chuckled. "I can't imagine a more inappropriate word but then why are we called gay, when most of the time we aren't? But that's a whole other story. You will tell me if all this talk bothers you, won't you?"

I nodded. "Ronnie, can I ask you something?

"Course you can."

"What does it feel like? Being, you know, the way you are."

"A poof? A queer? A homo?"

I cringed.

"It's OK, you can say it. I've heard all the words before. Well, how much time do we have? You know there are others like you because you've heard about them. People talking, or things in the news, but you feel totally alone, as if you're the only one in the whole, wide world. Back then I didn't know of any others like me, even though they were out there."

"So how do you stay so cheerful? You always seem to be happy enough."

"I am. But, like you, it's been a journey. One of the biggest things is that you look like everyone else so it makes it easy to hide. And you know that any of them could hate your guts for it and so you feel you need to hide it. You even fear your parents."

"But Stella and Freddie love you. Surely they would support you no matter what?"

"Easy to say but, until you try them, you just never know how they're going to respond, so you end up trusting no-one; no-one. Not even the people you should be able to trust most. Will they kick you out of the house, like lots of parents do? Nobody wants that, so they keep it hidden and it eats at you and eats at you." He sighed and gave me a mournful sideways glance. "I tell you, Sophe, those were desperate times and that pretty much applies to all of us homos. Just about all of us have been to hell and back. Most of us make it back. Some of us don't. Some of us deal with it and others just hide it away. Get married, have kids and sneak away for sex in the bushes or the public toilets, like those blokes we just saw. I know a few of them. It's hard for them, leading a double life. It's fucking exhausting, actually. I can tell you that for free. I bet you're sorry you asked now, aren't you?"

"No," I said. "I want to understand. I want to understand you."

"Oh, you will - especially if you move into the flat. But I think the biggest thing that we have to deal with is the fact that we can be totally inconspicuous and so it's easy for us to hide our real selves, which isn't a good thing. I mean when you're black there's no hiding it. You have to deal with it, and all the bigots, and there's plenty of those right now with all this immigration from the West Indies getting everybody worked up. They know the taste of discrimination alright."

"There's no avoiding it for them."

"That's right. All minorities are conspicuous in one way or another, except us queers. But the biggest thing that no other minority has to face is fear of their families. Now, I ask you, who else has to do that - except you, of course, so you get it. But think about it. Your parents are straight and so they're almost certainly bigoted against poofs so they'll most likely turn on you and who the hell wants that? They're supposed to love and protect you, right? But, instead, they eat you alive. I mean black families love and support their black kids and Jewish families do the same for Jewish kids. They don't say 'What do you mean you're a kike or a nigger? Get the fuck out of my house!' do they? Everyone in the world expects to get love and support from their family except the likes of us, and that can really screw you up, Sophe, believe you me. *And*, even if they don't kick you out, they want to fix you. They freak out and worry and try and get your head examined. Honest to god, I'm not sure what would be worse! I'm so bloody lucky with mum. And even that took some hard work."

"Your mum has been brilliant, but I'm sure it can't be easy dealing with it on her own and trying to keep your father out of it. Do you think he would freak out if he knew?" I asked.

Ronnie paused for a moment and we both stared across the green parkland. Families were enjoying themselves. Dads were throwing balls for their kids, flying kites, or pushing tricycles. Mums were holding toddlers and pushing prams.

"See those dads over there? The last thing they ever, *ever* want to hear when their sons are all grown up is that one of them is a nancy boy. That's absolutely the last thing they want to hear. They haven't got a clue how to deal with it and it's the last thing in the world they want for their son, or daughter for that matter, or for themselves. My dad is no exception, so I think that, as long as he doesn't know about it, he can avoid it. Mothers on the other hand need to know, don't you think? Even if they wring their hands and tear their hair out."

"I suppose so. But I probably won't understand that until

I become a mother, if that ever happens. Tell the truth, being a mother doesn't fill me with enthusiasm, based on what I've seen so far. I think that if my child was homosexual, I would want to know and help, but that's probably because I know you and understand it now."

"Of course it is. You know about this stuff now but how many ever do? The other thing is the feeling of isolation. Even though you might get used to the idea of who you are and how you have to live your life, you end up an outsider. You don't live life the same way as everybody else. You don't get married and raise families like everybody else, or socialize with your family and friends or go to school functions with all your kids' mums and dads. You don't see life the same way and then, before you realize it, you feel like you're on a different planet.

That's why we like to hang out with our own kind. We can relate to each other, understand what makes each other tick, empathize with all the bruises we got when we tried to come out of the closet. No-one else can do that and so there's a certain camaraderie. We create our own families where we can be safe and all be ourselves together. It's the one place that we can actually belong and I don't know if it'll ever change. Wouldn't it be great if it did? All those families out there, playing on the grass. I don't really relate to any of them. They're like a different species to me now. Does that make sense?"

"I suppose so," I said but, honestly, I was struggling. "I don't think anyone can really understand if they haven't been there themselves. It's just impossible."

We looked at all those supposedly happy families. "Can you imagine the world being different and some of those parents being two men or two women?"

"Pfff! That'll never happen," Ronnie said brusquely. "But you're right, you probably understand better than most because you've been to the edge; but you'll never feel like an outcast. You fit in. You're pretty, intelligent and, eventually, you'll want a husband and family. You are the classic conventional woman. But you know, Sophe, I'm glad for you because I wouldn't wish my situation on anyone. Some people say it offers some compensation but that's just the crumbs off the table while everyone else is enjoying the feast. But that's enough about me. What about you? You're still a teenager and still a virgin, am I right? Or did that pig of a father ever touch you?" Ronnie said sternly.

I didn't say anything. I was torn between continuing the lie and telling the truth. I was almost ready to open up to someone and Ronnie would be the easiest of all to confide in.

God knows the burden of it was crushing me.

But once it was out, it was out.

Like the genie in the bottle, I would never be able to get it back in and then what?

What are the consequences?

For me.

For my mother.

For my father.

For my future.

For everything.

My whole world.

And the shame of it.

The confusion.

The fear.

I just didn't know if now was the right time to be vulnerable again.

"Yes, I was afraid of that. Your silence tells me everything but I'm not going to ask you again and I'm not going to say anything to anyone. You can tell me in your own time. I want to help. Really I do. We've both had bad starts but we can work on that because, honestly, there's a lot to enjoy. Without going into detail that might embarrass us both right now, I can tell you that sex can be the best thing in the world and you will definitely want to enjoy it, especially when you're doing it with someone you love. That's something that money just can't buy. Trust me on that one. But I guess that's going to have to be part of your education. In the meantime, you make sure you study those books Ellen gave you and remind me to give you my copy of 'Lady Chatterley's Lover' and find out what all the excitement's about."

Ronnie came over and put his arm around me and I leant into his shoulder. It was comforting. "I will be able to talk about it. Just not yet."

"That's fine. In your own time." He hugged me tight. "And speaking of Ellen, let's go home and see if those two layabouts are up. I reckon a hair of the dog at 'The Dancing Bear' would be a good idea this lunch time, along with a nice basket of scampi and chips. What do you say? Sound like a good idea? And, in the meantime, let's get an ice cream," he said, pointing to the ice cream van at the entrance to the common. "My big treat! C'mon, let's go. And, talking of good ideas, think about what I said. I can get you a job in no time. In fact, I think there's somebody leaving the main office soon, to have a baby. It could work perfectly."

And it did.

It had been a wonderful party and now the fun was over.

17

Sophia Starts the 9 to 5

Sophia's story...

I READ MY BOOKS AND BOUGHT 'Cosmopolitan' every month. I now knew what lovemaking looked like, and was learning how women were behaving, thinking and changing in the swinging sixties. It was all very tantalizing and I was readying myself to participate. It felt like a golden age for women like me and my generation. Even the generation that went before were getting a taste of it, those that weren't already immersed in the subservient, patriarchal family society, where men always knew best, regardless of whether they did or not, and where women held to their place for the good of the family and the ego of the husband.

"Darling, men are pigs and ripe for the slaughterhouse, but women just don't have a taste for that much blood," Ellen said to me one day over a shandy. "But I think more and more of us are getting ready to skewer them now that we're learning to take our freedom."

She was right, of course, and I stuck to my determination to keep my distance from all men emotionally until I was fully equipped to take them on as an equal or - as Ellen would say - a superior. I was still young but it wasn't difficult to figure out that there were two different kinds of love and men - the destructive and the constructive. I had grown up with the former and had seen it all around me and, now that I was living with Stella and Freddie, I could see the latter in all its glory.

I liked that one.

That was my pick.

The love of family, of shared experience, affection, companionship. It all seemed so calm and welcoming after the froth and fury of hostilities that I had lived with once the scales had fallen from my parents' eyes; when they both realised who they were stuck with for life because, back then, it was almost always for life.

A life sentence.

Not for me though – uh!uh!

So, I studied and read until my brain ached.

Meanwhile, Ronnie got me my interview with Miss Best, an elderly spinster who looked after the administration of the agency's head office, around the corner from Wimbledon railway station. Ronnie's good advice to dress conservatively and limit the makeup paid off. I was able to disarm her with my quiet politeness, because timid came easily to me as my natural behaviour.

I took the train to Wimbledon, making my way from the greenbelt edge of home to the bustling, grubby city's edge. Walking briskly and nervously past the storefronts and street traffic I reached the traditional windows of Witherby's & Co., filled with details of all types of houses and flats for sale. It all looked rather daunting, as did Miss Best when she strode through the main office to meet me with a rather forced smile. This would be my first real job, if I was to get it. Being a barmaid a few nights a week didn't count.

This time it was serious.

Adult stuff.

"Hello, Miss Foxton. I'm Miss Best. Come this way, won't you?"

I was led through the main showroom to a small office, tucked under the stairs, crammed with supplies and furnished with a small table and two chairs.

She was a plump, snowy-haired and drably dressed matron in flat shoes, who had clearly never experienced passion in her life or, if she had, it and its memory had long since departed. Despite the slightly sour look, she was pleasant enough and in good humour that day. I was hoping that Ronnie had been able to do some preparatory work with some gentle persuasion in my favour, so that she was well disposed to me already. I need not have worried on that score.

"This is my little private domain," she said as she laid her pad and pencil on the table and indicated for me to take the other chair. The room was panelled in dark wood, the table and chairs equally cheerless. A small white lampshade over the hanging light bulb was the only thing of softness in the tiny room.

"Ronald has told me a quite a lot about you already and, first of all, let me say how sorry I am to hear about the death of your parents. That must have been very hard for you. I lost my father when I was young as well and that was very hard, but to lose both must be so much worse."

I smiled wanly, slightly ashamed of the lie.

"Thank you. The situation with my parents has been quite traumatic but Ronnie - I mean Ronald's - parents have been wonderful to me." None of that was a lie and I hoped to get the subject changed without having to. Lying was one thing I refused to do wherever possible because it did not come naturally to me. I was convinced they would always, eventually, catch me out. "Ronald's mother is my mother's sister and she's treated me like her own. I've been very fortunate."

"Ronald's such a nice young man and such a hard worker. He's highly regarded at Witherby's, as I'm sure you know." This time she smiled more broadly and I could tell that Ronnie had worked his magic here too. This shouldn't be so difficult after all, I thought, and started to relax. She's going to want to hire me to keep Ronnie happy, I thought, as it quickly became apparent how soft a spot she had for him.

"Ronnie tells me that you've completed a secretarial course and are looking for a position that will allow you to improve your shorthand and typing skills. Well, you've come to the right place. We have a group of girls here that do nothing but typing up particulars and survey reports. Attention to detail is critical because they all go out to the public and need to be as close to perfect as possible. Reports are done in triplicate and, as you know, corrections are time-consuming. We have some good girls here and, if you're up to scratch, I'm sure you'll fit in. The men in the front office can be a bit snooty. Most of them think they have some special gifts or something, but I think most of us women here could do as good, and probably better," she declared and sniffed. "They say women will never make estate agents. Too emotional, they say. But I say that's exactly what they need." She rolled her eyes. "But I don't see it ever changing."

"How long have you been here, Miss Best?"

"Oh, my dear, I've been here since I started working over forty years ago. First I was in the typing pool like you. Then I became secretary to Mr. Witherby Senior before the war. He was the founding Mr. Witherby. He's the 'since 1905' that you see on our window. Then, when he retired after the war, I became the next Mr. Witherby's secretary and I've been doing that ever since. Mr. Witherby Junior runs the city office now. They've all been very nice. Very professional. Mr. Witherby Senior will probably be retiring in a few years and I will probably stay on with him until then and then retire myself." She flashed me a knowing smile and said pointedly, "So there will be opportunity."

Opportunity?

Call that an opportunity?

I thought it all sounded like my worst nightmare, yet Miss Best seemed to have been satisfied, but at what cost? What choice did this woman have some forty years ago, I asked myself? What control over her destiny?

Here I was, a child of the swinging sixties, bursting with choices as everyone fought for their own sense of freedom and individuality, pushing determinedly away from their parents' conventions. And here she was, after forty years of serving three generations of the same family. Working in the same office, probably living in the same miserable little house. Here she still was, eking out a living from one dull week to the next, caring for an aging parent no doubt, with no-one's love or affection to soften the harshness of that cold, dull, tedious routine.

She continued. "The only thing I regret is that I have never been able to do more than be someone's assistant. I'm too old and set in my ways to change now, but women like you are entering a whole new world where they can actually take control of their lives. You, and others like you, are going to be very lucky, I think. You'll be able to create your own destiny." She smiled and patted my hand.

My eyes widened. Had she been reading my thoughts? 'Don't be like me,' was what she was really saying. We talked about the office and the business. I was able to talk meaningfully about things after spending so much time with Ronald and she could tell that I had intelligence enough to spare.

Quickly it became clear to her that I was a safe bet and because I was clearly cut from the same cloth as Ronald. The conversation turned into a surprisingly honest chat about her spinsterhood, lost love and years spent looking after an invalid mother. Ah-hah! I was right! She was clearly the sort of woman I hoped never to become.

Despite the outer shield of stiffness, she seemed more warm-hearted and kind than I first imagined, but she was tied up in the social conventions of a society that was rapidly changing and her world did not much resemble the world that I planned to inhabit.

After an hour, Miss Best neatly drew our conversation to a close. "Well, the job's yours if you want it. It'll last as long as Sybil is away having her baby but, if you ask me, she won't be back and, even if she is, we can find you something permanent, I'm sure. Especially if you're willing to move to one of our other offices."

I beamed. "Thank you. I would love it. When do you want me to start?"

"Next week?"

18

A Home of My Own

Sophia's story...

THE FIRST FEW WEEKS, I TOOK the train from my home at Stella and Freddie's. Then Ellen moved out of Ronnie's flat and I moved in. Even though most of the furniture and household bits and pieces were Ronnie's I was excited beyond belief that I had my own place, or as close to one as I was going to get for a while. It was my address, my phone number and now my own rules. Unless I stepped out of line, no-one was going to tell me what, when or how to do anything and I could hardly believe it.

Thanks to Ronnie's good taste – "most poofs have it" he was in the habit of saying. "It's something we're born with so that we can compensate for the dreary homes we grew up in." – the flat was bright and smart and furnished with simple, modern furniture that was becoming all the rage. The flat was painted white, except the kitchen and bathroom which were both painted bright orange, and the parquet floors were exposed and layered with colourful, abstract rugs.

"God bless mum and dad," he exclaimed when I asked how he could afford to furnish it. "And I have a friend in the business, thank god. A very good friend, if you know what I mean." He winked.

It was lovely and I felt at home from the moment I moved in. Ronnie had learnt how to cook, albeit a limited repertoire, so I never wanted for a good meal. I loved spending my time there, with or without Ronnie. I spent time walking on the Common and exploring the shops and boutiques along the High Street. I started to become recognised as a local as people acknowledged me in the street. For the first time in my short life, I began to feel at home; to recognise and appreciate what that felt like. The warm pleasure of it.

It was so far removed from the Croydon council estate where I had spent most of my life that I had to pinch myself frequently to be sure that this really was me and this really was where I was. My greatest fear was that I would wake up one day to find it had all been just a dream.

I moved all my things into the flat one Saturday afternoon in late October and Freddie and Stella helped me to take the suitcases over and settle me in. After they left, Ronnie offered to make dinner and prepared spaghetti Bolognese. I still wasn't used to foreign food and each time was a novelty and surprise.

"I've got a nice, cheap bottle of Italian plonk here to go with the meal. Makes it a bit of a celebration, and why not?"

We sat in the warm light of table lamps in the sitting room as the sauce was slowly bubbling, and had our first glass. "I hate overhead lamps, don't you? They give such an awful light; sucks the atmosphere out of any room. Cheers!" as we clinked glasses. "So, here you are, Miss

Independent! Finally on your own, living your own life on your own terms. How does it feel? Scary?" Ronnie asked, sipping his wine.

"Sort of. I keep thinking it's all going to fall apart and that I'll end up back where I started from, but that fear is fading now."

"Good, because that's never going to happen. The spinster of this parish seems to have taken a shine to you, so that'll help you lots."

"Who?"

"The spinster of this parish - our Miss Best. Miss 'never been kissed'. We've got a few names for her, all of them cruel."

I frowned in disapproval.

"I know. It's wrong and we should know better but you know life - pick on the weakest before they all pick on you. She's too easy a target - plain Jane with no life to speak of. But she has a good heart and, to be fair, I've gone out of my way to be nice to her because, firstly, she deserves it and, secondly, it takes one to know one and, as an outsider myself, I empathize with her."

"Well, that's paid off because she definitely has a soft spot for you. Is she a lesbian, do you think?" My curiosity had gotten the better of me.

"Honestly? I don't think she is. I just think she got left behind. Probably had a few boyfriends, then the war came, then her mother was widowed and she's spent the rest of her life comforting her. She's probably had an unrequited yearning for Mr. Witherby Senior and - wham bam - before you know it, it's gotten you nowhere and you've become all shrivelled up and old, and it's all too late. Seen it time and time again. She's the old style of woman and you're the new."

We sat down to our dinner, sipped more wine and talked on into the evening.

"Anyway, how are you enjoying the new job?"

"I like it. It's a bit boring, just being in the typing pool but I've started to get to know some of the girls, and some of the negotiators; getting to know more of what goes on. I like all the different properties that come in and all the different people that they deal with. I could see myself getting quite interested in all that."

"Trouble is, that's the man's world. You've probably noticed that, unless you wear trousers, you don't get to do any of that," Ronnie smiled wistfully. "We need to get some change happening there, to get you more involved. Maybe we can get you to another office some time, even if it's just part time, where they're not so set in their ways and the management is younger."

"They definitely like you. I reckon you'll be a partner one day if you keep it up," I said quietly, for effect.

"You think so?"

"Of course!" I exclaimed" Surely you can see that, can't you?"

"Too close to it. I can't read it very well when it's that personal. That's my problem. And talking of work and partners, have you met Mr. Witherby Junior?"

"I've seen him a few times, passing through the office. He seems a bit of a snob. Nose in the air and barely a glimpse in anyone's direction. I didn't take to him much."

"Well, you'd probably be a bit of a snob too with his private schools and parents in high places. Mr. Senior is much more friendly and relaxed but he worked his way up and Mr. Junior was born with the silver spoon. They don't just own the chain of estate agents, you know. They've been busy buying property all around the south-west of London - especially the first Mr. Witherby - when it was cheap after the First World War and then Mr. Senior after the second world war. Now they've got quite the portfolio. You're living in one," Ronnie laughed. "And when they're both gone, Mr. Junior and Miss Junior get to inherit the lot."

"Who's Miss Junior?" I asked.

"She's the daughter. But she's married and living in Cornwall with a painter, so she's pretty much out of the picture. She'll take the money and run when the time comes, but Junior will be working the farm, so to speak. He's going to be taking all the property and the business and growing it even more. You should try and get your foot in that door, Sophe! He's got a girlfriend I think, but she's been around for a while and nothing has happened although I hear it might very soon so you'd better get your skates on."

We sipped our wine as we finished our spaghetti.

Ronnie picked up the conversation again.

"Something about him is setting off my jungle drums. I don't know what it is but I get the feeling that he might be one of the lads. Don't repeat this to a soul. It's just a feeling I've got and I can't be sure, but something doesn't sit right."

"So you think he might prefer Ronnie to Rhonda? You should be making eyes at him, not me."

"Maybe I should," Ronnie laughed. "I wouldn't be the first employee to shag the boss to get a promotion. But somehow I don't see myself becoming part of that family no matter how nice I am and how good a job I do. You, on the other hand…"

Ronnie winked and disappeared to the kitchen, returning with two delicious looking chocolate eclairs and two steaming cups of coffee, placing them on the dining table close to the window where we had been sitting for the past hour, watching the world go by.

"Did I tell you who was in our office last Thursday, looking for a house? Toby Winters!" Ronnie exclaimed.

"What, Toby Winters the actor?"

"Yes, the very same. With his 'friend'. 'I'm looking for a large house close to the Common, he said. My friend is coming along to help me make up my mind,' he said. 'Yeah, right! I wanted to say," and Ronnie smirked. "I could tell right away what he was doing there. Don't tell me that he wasn't going to be living there and sharing his bedroom with his so-called friend."

I squirmed. Talk like that still made me uncomfortable. I was, it seemed, still a long way from enlightenment.

"Anyway, I got him first so I'm going to be handling him, if you know what I mean," he said and leered at me. "God! I would love to handle him. He's even better looking in person than he is on the screen. And I can imagine why he wants to be close to the Common, so that he can pick up tricks in the bushes like the rest of them."

"What do you mean, pick up tricks?"

"It's what the lads do when they get randy and want a quick - how shall I put this - release. Like those two men we saw on the heath. They stroll around certain parts of the Common looking for other lads with a similar need. Eyes meet, one thing leads to another, they have their bit of bump and grind and maybe, maybe not, see each other again or go hunting for someone new the next time. It's fun for some."

"God, it doesn't sound much like fun to me."

"It can be." Ronnie replied tellingly. "But few people can understand that. It sounds way too perverted for most people to stomach. But a lot of men like the thrill and the excitement of it and, in some strange way, I can see why. There's just no accounting for taste, is there? Pick a deviation and there's always someone ready to indulge in it. Incidentally, talking of deviations, have you been studying Ellen's books? Now they should be an eye-opener. Maybe I should be studying them after you. Give me some new ideas."

"I have and you're right. They are an eye opener. Honestly, I can't imagine my mum and dad, or your mum and dad for that matter, doing any of that stuff, but I suppose they must have."

"Probably still do," whispered Ronnie.

"Eeew! I don't want to think about that. I wouldn't mind trying it out with Stephen Cyrus though. You know, the tall dark-haired man in my office."

"Old Stevie? Really? Does he turn your crank then? Doesn't do it for me but then we all like different things." He winked. "And in different places. He's too fond of himself, if you ask me. Although I suppose I can see the attraction. I'm not crazy about men who love themselves more than anyone else but, heck, he could be good practice. What do you think about Anthony? Now he'd be good practice. I'd throw myself over him except he's not into his own kind."

"You mean, Anthony Rogers? The gigolo, as he calls himself?"

"Yeah. That's the one, although he's not really a gigolo. He just says that for effect. Gigolos do it for money. He does it for fun and, of course, as much power and influence as he can get. Doctor to the rich and famous. Fancy address. Big fees. So, yes, I suppose he has done it for money! Good thing he's a nice bloke or he probably would have come undone by now."

I could tell Ronnie was giving this more thought and that this was not to be the end of it.

"I suspect he could give you quite an education," he mused, almost absent-mindedly then turned to me and smiled. "So, do you want to watch a bit of telly before bed? You can have 'Coronation Street' or 'Steptoe & Son'. Depends if you want to laugh or cry, or both. And one day soon, I'll get a colour TV. Wouldn't that be nice for the wet, dark winter evenåings?"

Very cozy, I thought.

19

Sadness and Sorrow Part 1

Ronnie's story...

A DEAR FRIEND DIED TODAY. It was a sad day, made worse by the fact that I did not know how to deal with death because I had never had to before.

How do you deal with the death of someone you never thought would die? Yes, of course, one day they would but, at the age of twenty-five, the thought never crosses your mind and then - bang - one day they're gone and you have no chance to prepare.

But do you ever prepare for death?

Doesn't it just happen and then, only afterwards, do you know if it will pass with a sad but disconnected sense of loss? Or will it gnaw your insides until you can't stand it anymore?

This was somewhere in between, made worse by the fact that it was tragic. Simon his name was, and he used to be my boyfriend. Not for long, but long enough to love him enough to not want to lose him. So, even when it was over between us, we remained friends, as so often happens in this underworld of uncertain liaisons.

Staying connected.

Remaining friends.

Being there for each other.

Our break-up was neat, tidy, clean. But the next one wrecked him because of the intensity of it all. He was head over heels in a one-sided romance and they're the worst, aren't they?

It always shows.

All over you.

No matter how hard you try.

Even the passengers on the bus can see you're a quivering wreck from the intoxication of it; like the shakes.

The obsession.

Will he call?

Won't he?

And so you wait for the axe to fall.

The love to die.

The misery to descend.

Bad love.

Bad, bad love.

We all get some, some time, don't we?

Poor bastard.

And this was his turn.

And him in a family that didn't know and would never understand, so there was no-one to talk to about the pain. Just mooching about the house with his chin on the floor and no-one daring to ask what's wrong for fear of finding out the truth. But, of course, the truth will out and, in time, he was the shame of the family.

Unwelcome.

Reviled.

A stain to be removed.

Rejected.

Ejected.

Alone and, of course, suicidal.

And bridges are everywhere in London, aren't they?

An easy escape.

One jump and it's almost over.

A few more minutes and it is.

I got the call from a friend, who had heard from another friend and, that very evening, we gathered at a queer friendly pub in the city for an informal wake where we could all get drunk and cry and nobody cared except us. Which is what we did, right there amongst the shabby, smoke-laden red velvet and scuffed mahogany. We all mourned the loss of another queer brother, lost to the cause.

"Should we go to the funeral then?"

"Why wouldn't we?"

"Because they hate us."

"They don't know us."

"They'll know us alright, and then they'll hate us."

"But we're going?"

"We're going."

"It's not for them we're going. The ignorant fuckers. It's for him. It's for Simon. The boy in the box. The boy who should still be enjoying his life except his fucking family put a stop to that. The miserable bastards."

"So what's new?"

We had another drink for the dead boy.

My boy.

Our boy.

We mourned into our beer and wondered if one of us could - would - end up the same.

"Those bastards might as well have pushed him off the bridge for all the damage they did. Call themselves parents. Murderers more like."

It was all bile and bitterness borne out of personal experience and we drowned our sorrows before hugs and tears all around as we said our fond farewells. Plans were made to reunite at the funeral.

God, was I shit-faced, and I mean shit-faced. All the demons from my past bought me a drink that night and, laughing, had made me swig them down, all in one long gulp.

Hanging over the edge of the platform of Wimbledon tube station, it all came back up. A foul brew made more bitter by the thoughts in my head. The dregs of it clung to me - serve me right - as I staggered home and stumbled through the front door, crying, as I recall.

Sophia came to my rescue and got the whole story as she held me and wiped my face. Friends are family, aren't they? More than family, because they accept you as you are, not as they want you to be.

I was mad at the world.

We both got mad at the world.

We cried together and then we went to bed.

I was fucking exhausted.

And then there was the funeral.

It all went well until we left the church and paid our respects to the family. That's when it turned ugly. There were eight of us altogether, including Peter, Ellen and Sophia, who didn't know Simon but came along for moral support. Simon's family didn't know any of us but they suspected the worst simply based on the fact that we were the best looking, best dressed group there - bar none.

If we're going to be pariahs, we might as well do it with style.

We followed the other mourners out of the church and prepared to give our condolences to Simon's mother and father. We could feel the tension, but that was nothing compared to the reaction.

"You don't know us," I said on everyone's behalf. "We were friends of Simon."

Simon's father talked first, although hissed is more the word. "You don't need to tell us who you are." He spat the words. "You're the bunch of perverts who ruined my son. I don't know how you have the nerve to show up here today and make a joke of this whole bloody funeral."

"We're only here to …" Ellen started, already getting heated.

"To what? Make an exhibition of yourselves? Rub our noses in it? You should be bloody ashamed of yourself. I don't know how you lot have got the nerve." He was sobbing now and his wife was standing to one side, wiping her eyes and looked as if she wanted to crawl into the coffin alongside her son, but I could not tell if it was through grief or embarrassment.

Peter pulled Ellen by the arm and herded all of us away. There was no hope for us here. No way of crossing this great divide. Yet, as we moved away through the churchyard and towards the street, Sophia turned back and we watched her go to Simon's mother, take her hand and talk to her. Close like confidantes.

She smiled wanly while her husband was snapping at her heels like a terrier. Finally, Sophia turned to him and, with her face barely inches from his, spoke to him sharply. You couldn't make out the words but the reaction was instantaneous. She had his full attention and they spoke for a moment before she turned on her heels and joined us.

We were speechless.

"Don't ask." She was quivering and, by now, tearful from all the sudden emotion that had taken a lot out of her, I could tell.

She was going to need a drink.

We all were.

And that's precisely what we had.

20

Sadness and Sorrow Part 2

Sophia's story...

Peter pulled us away from the mourners and led us down the churchyard path but I couldn't go. I couldn't let what had happened just lie there like poison. Not on a day like this. So I turned back and moved towards Simon's mother, much to her husband's fury.

When I returned to my party, they were agog.

"What did you say?"

"I just took her hand and I told her something you once told me, Ronnie, that I've always remembered. 'God is never going to judge anyone for who they love, only for who they hate,' I said, 'so please don't ever think badly of your son because of who he loved.'

"I didn't know you were so religious."

"I'm not, but she probably is. And then I asked him why fathers were often so hateful to the ones they were supposed to love the most."

"Well, that certainly shut him up."

"That wasn't my intention. I just wanted to show some sympathy to his wife who was grieving for the loss of her son and ashamed of her husband's behaviour. You could see it in her face. She just wanted to be swallowed up. It was tragic. Look at her. She's in another world."

We turned back and, yes, she was lost.

Lost to this world.

Hopefully, she would find a way back but, for now, there was no hope. I was determined to help her and so I wrote her a letter, to which she replied.

And I wrote her another one, asking if I could visit her. And she said yes. I was afraid that she might have no-one to confide in. She might have plenty of family and friends, or she might not. But they would not be the people to confide in. To talk about your innermost fears, hurts, despair. They'll just tell you to cheer up and give you a nice cuppa tea. I was worried for her. I may have been young, naïve and didn't know much, but one thing I knew was that this was hurting her badly.

Very badly indeed.

Three weeks after the funeral, I visited her in her neat terraced Victorian house in Putney. All red brick and a tidy front garden, behind a low stone wall and wrought iron fence, it was typical of thousands like it all over London. It reminded me of Anita's except that this street - this house - had aspirations and a bright red front door. Brilliant, dazzling red gloss that looked recently applied and made it stand out from its neighbours.

I rang the bell and waited for quite some time before the door opened. I guessed from her red and puffy eyes that she had to get herself under control first.

"Hello, Mrs. Carpenter." I smiled and paused. I was at a loss. Giving comfort to others was new to me and I was stumbling. "I love your front door," was all I could say.

She forced a slight smile, "Simon's idea. Now when I

come home I remember him. As if I could forget. Come on in, dear."

She ushered me into the front room, bright with the sunshine through the net curtains and turning the floral wallpaper into an almost glowing landscape. The swirling patterns of the carpet combined to create something that was more like a kaleidoscope than a room. And it was spotlessly clean. Everything shone, except her.

"I've boiled the kettle. I'll make a nice cup of tea, shall I?"

"Lovely."

And then she was gone. I was left to look at the photographs scattered about the room, on the mantelpiece, the sideboard, on shelves. Family photographs of holidays and outings to the seaside. The earlier ones were always of two children but the more recent ones were just of a boy who became a young man whom I assumed was Simon, some with and some without his mother and father.

But who was the girl who disappeared, I wondered?

Mrs. Carpenter returned with a tray. Two cups of tea, milk jug, sugar bowl and a plate of assorted biscuits. You only had to look at the tray to know you were in England.

"I'll let you help yourself. Then you'll have it just the way you want it."

"Thanks." I paused. "I was looking at the photos. You've got so many nice ones. That must be Simon, is it? He's very handsome. Even as a child."

"Yes, too handsome for his own good, we used to say. Get you into trouble one day, we said. Not knowing how true that would be."

"Mrs. Carpenter, I don't want to intrude but I really want to try and help. I know this is an awful time but I thought you might want someone to talk to. Someone outside your usual circle, you know, even if it is a kid like me. But please say if I ask too much or if you have had enough of me."

"It's alright, love. Tell the truth, it's lovely to have someone to talk to who doesn't know anything about us. Just to let it out. You might regret it," she said with a weak smile. "But, yes, he was a lovely lad. Lovely. Everybody used to comment. Never got into any trouble. Teachers all liked him and he always got good reports. He was the first one in the family to go to University. But then he got all moody. He'd come home for holidays and you could barely get a peep out of him. 'Course he missed his sister but that wasn't the problem, although I thought it was."

"That must be her in the photographs? She's pretty too."

I picked up one that showed her with Simon and his mother. He was kneeling down under a bright blue sky on what must have been a glorious summer day. He was looking straight at the camera with a dazzling smile and his sister was looking at him and laughing. Their mother was looking at both of them with a look of quiet detachment, a light pencil-stroke of a smile on her face as she admired what she had; what made her happy.

Clearly, it was her family that made her happy and it showed.

"What's her name?" I asked.

"June," she smiled, paused and added, "And mine is May and my sister's is April. April came first, then me, then June. Family joke." She smiled feebly, as her lower lip quivered. "And I'm the only one left now."

I turned pale. This was going to be difficult and I didn't know if I was up for it.

"You mean …?"

"Yes, that's what I mean. Both dead now. Sister and daughter and now my son. Back to square one. Been a mother all my life, Sophia, and now I'm not. You're too young to understand what that feels like but it feels like someone ripped my heart out and threw it away. It's not a pain. It's an ache. A huge, gnawing ache that won't go away and sadness that just won't let up. Honest to God, Sophia, if Simon felt anything like I feel, then I know how easy it must have been for him to do what he did. You just want it over with."

"What happened?"

"They were both killed in an accident about five years ago. June was staying with her Auntie April and they were out in the car when a lorry hit them. I thought I would die then but I pulled through and now this." She looked at me pitifully, tears brimming. "You grow up planning to get married and be a mother. You get married and start planning for a family. Then you become a mother and that's what your life is and you think about being a grandmother. That's a woman's life, Sophia, and it can be a wonderful life, as I'm sure you'll find out one day. Watching them grow. Nurturing them and dreaming about what will become of them and then, when they go like this, it's like your whole life has been for nothing, or might as well have been for all the good it is now. Even the memories turn bitter." She looked at me with sheer despair. "Please, god, I hope that changes."

I was struggling to hold back the tears myself. I had not bargained for this. Giving myself a psychological slap, I told myself that I was there for her and the last thing she needed was for me to fall apart. I sipped my tea.

"And how did your husband cope with it?"

She laughed sharply. "Well, he didn't have much time for my sister. A flibbertigibbet he called her. He didn't like women to be all full of life and cheeky so she wasn't to his taste, but she was a sweetheart and I was very fond her. She helped raise me after all, so we were very close. But Andrew - my husband - didn't take to her much so he had the ideal person to blame for losing June, even though it wasn't her fault. He needs someone to blame and that's why your lot got it in the neck at the funeral." She paused and took a sip of her tea. "I could have died that day. The way he treated you and, I'm sorry, I just couldn't say anything or it would have just been worse."

"He must be shattered."

"Yes, he is. That's a good word for it. When June died it was awful. Awful! I thought I'd lose him an' all. He was so low. Drinking too much. Out on his own, just walking. Brooding. And I was at home doing the same thing but he didn't think of that, did he?" Her voice was as sharp as a razor blade for a moment, before softening again. "And now here we are again! Another child dead and I'm afraid of how it's going to end this time."

We both sat in silence for a moment, looking at the photographs, sipping tea and gathering thoughts.

"You know what the worst thing about this is?"

"No. Please tell me."

"The shame. Our son is dead and it's not bad enough that he killed himself but he was also homosexual. There, I've said it. Do you know that through all this mess no-one has used that word? Nobody. Not us. Not me. Not friends nor family. They can't bring themselves to say it and Andrew is so ashamed of it that it's eating him up. If Simon had been a child murderer I think Andrew would have felt better about it. Can you imagine? Burying your own son and being ashamed of him? And why? Because … because he was just being who he was!" She sobbed and for several minutes we sat there as she let it go. "I could kill him myself for that. I really could. How dare he curse his own son on his deathbed and for what? For just being himself?" She choked back bitter tears. "But my dear husband doesn't see it that way," she hissed.

Mrs. Carpenter was distraught and I moved across to comfort her, to put my arm around her as she sobbed. Funny, I thought. My mother had sobbed many times in our house. In my presence. All I did was turn my back on her, disgusted and disappointed. And, just then, through a crack in the memory of it all, I saw her just like May.

Lost.

Alone.

Wretched.

Needing sympathy that I was determined to refuse her.

"If it had been June that had been jilted and all miserable we would have all rallied round for her, but not for Simon. We all recoiled in horror and disgust and now look at the mess."

"He never confided in you?"

"Oh, god! No! Those things never get talked about, do they? But, of course, subconsciously I knew. I had an inkling of where Simon was going from a young boy but I couldn't put two and two together without making six. Now, in hindsight, it's all so clear. I just wish I had been clever enough to recognise it and help him before it all turned sour."

"It's not an easy thing to do." I said. "It always seems to be so well-hidden. If it wasn't for my cousin Ronnie, who you met at the church, I would be completely clueless. Most people are. I suppose they try and keep it that way, for their own safety."

"Safety? That's a joke! Not much safety in that as far as I can tell. And now look at the mess! What a bloody awful mess. Now I have to try and clean it up because Andrew won't, I know that much." She paused and looked directly at me. "You know what. When I saw that coffin go into the ground, I could have jumped in after it and they could have covered me in dirt and I would have been the happiest woman alive. Just me and Simon. Dead together. And the rest of the world can go to hell."

She wailed now and it was a tragic sight wrapped in a desperate noise.

I felt myself growing years older as I sat there learning

more than I wanted to about the grim realities of our existence, while feeling helpless and hopeless. My young life, and all its miserable history, was inconsequential to what May had been through and I felt as useless to help her as I had the minute I walked in.

I was damaged but she was ruined.

As she sat there, her head in her hands, I opened up like never before about what I had gone through and we hugged and cried. Strangers in need of comfort that we were ready and willing to give.

"We all get damaged in different ways, don't we?" she sighed. "It's never easy. We're always fighting something or someone, especially us women. But even that's changing now, and not before time either. We've all been cowering from our men folk for far too long - and I'm one of the lucky ones! Despite what you might think, Andrew has a good heart - or had. It just needs some mending. He'll never live with himself in years to come, looking back on this time and how he behaved. How he soured it all and poisoned his own son's memory." She sighed and looked at me with a thin smile. "Just remember this when you're a mother, Sophia. Treasure your children always because you never know when they'll be gone. We take too much for granted."

"I'm not sure I'm mother material. I'm damaged goods, remember."

"You're young, luv! You have plenty of time to recover and, besides, there's plenty more been where you've been and still come out the other side OK."

I laughed. The first laugh of the afternoon. "Promise? And, if I do, I just might ask you to be a godmother, if you're willing?"

"Don't make promises you can't keep." She smiled through her snuffles. "You're a lovely girl and you have a good heart. You keep it safe. One day you'll make somebody very happy and there'll be a queue a mile long for the chance, you mark my words, what with your looks. You've got all your life to get it right, so no point making a sudden mistake."

There was a sense of kindred spirits in the room and we talked openly and honestly about all sorts of things until it was time to go.

"I don't want to kick you out but Andrew will be home soon and I don't want to have another confrontation. I couldn't handle it."

"Of course. I'll go now but can we keep in touch? I really liked our chance to talk and I hope we can do it again."

"Course we can. I'd like that. I really would." She gave me a hug. "And thank you for coming to see me. That means a lot to me, that does. And I'd like to meet Simon's friends one day too. I want to find out more about the son I had. You know, the hidden part. The things a mother should know but doesn't. At least not in a situation like this. I want to know that he'd been happy sometimes as well. I really, really hope I hear that. God knows, it's what a mother wants to know most of all."

We had met as strangers and parted as friends, or so it felt like to both of us.

"I'll write." I said.

And I did.

Often.

And, in time, she did become a godmother to my children.

Well, not exactly mine.

21

Sophia Has a Date

Sophia's story...

FOR ME, LIFE CONTINUED A PREDICTABLE path. I worked steadily at the office every weekday, taking the red double-decker bus into town, admiring the modest but comfortable middle-class activity going on around me and thanking whatever gods or fates were working for me over the past couple of years.

For others though, life was in turmoil.

The demonstrations against the Vietnam War were spreading further and wider but this was, of course, all lost on me. I focused on my life ahead, completely oblivious to the impact the Vietnam War and its life and death struggles would have on me, just beyond the horizon of the road that I was so determinedly travelling.

The hippies, meanwhile, were spreading their words of love and peace around the world and, along with it, sex, drugs and rock and roll. Women were demanding more and more, and getting it. Legalized abortion gave them a surge of power over their own bodies, setting off a maelstrom of controversy which, for decades and to this day, rages on in much the same way as LGBTQ rights.

For me though, life was good.

I loved my new home. Sharing it with Ronnie made me feel so safe and grounded. More than anything, it allowed me to live life closer to the edge than I otherwise ever would have, knowing I had someone by my side to catch me if I over-stepped.

But, for now, I was keeping a low profile, absorbing my surroundings and thinking about my future. At nineteen I had time on my side, but I was ready and willing to explore more. I was friendly with my co-workers and chummed up with a couple of the girls in the typing pool, and even had a drink or two with Stephen Cyrus.

He had attitude but I liked him, and he helped me understand more about the business we were in than I would ever pick up in the typing pool. I dressed modestly for the office but it was clear to everyone that I had some great assets that men would love to get their hands on.

Even down-playing my attractions, as in the less-is-more method, involved a degree of self-promotion which in some ways helped me more than if I was flaunting it. No-one could criticize me for being showy or flaunting anything. If men insisted on overlaying their fantasies on my otherwise respectable appearance, that was their problem, wasn't it?

I couldn't help it if men found me lovely to look at. It was a fine line to walk though, looking business-like to all my co-workers, male and female, while being secretly lusted after and talked about by the men - which, frankly, still scared me.

Stephen was one of those who lusted and, while not being pushy, was certainly flirtatious. Not surprisingly, one evening, as the office was closing at the end of a wet, cold day, and with Christmas around the corner, he took my arm and guided me to the pub at the corner.

"Let's get better acquainted," he said as he raised his umbrella to protect us both. "Besides, if you don't, you are going to get very wet."

"OK, but I can't stay long." I replied a bit too severely.

"Can't or won't?"

"I'm not sure yet," I said and turned to face him clearly with a half-smile. "That depends on how well you behave. I've heard stories in the typing pool. That's what we all talk about all day, you know, to keep us sane."

"What? Me? You all spend your time talking about me?" Stephen cried half-mockingly. "I'm flattered."

"Don't be. We talk about all of you and most of it isn't good." I laughed as Stephen pulled the pub door open and we ran in from the rain.

The interior was typical sixties town pub. Windows obscured so that passers-by wouldn't be shocked at the sight of people drinking, high ceilings and lots of red velvet curtains to which cigarette smoke clung like the devil's perfume. Stephen pulled out a chair at a small table in a quiet corner.

"What's your poison?"

"Shandy, please."

"Shandy it is. I'll be right back and don't go speaking to any strange men. At least none stranger than me," he smirked and disappeared to the bar.

As I waited, I looked around the room. It was busy, but not full, with a range of end-of-work-day men, some in overalls and some in suits or overcoats. There were a few women in the bar, mostly middle-aged, over-dressed and over-painted, laughing too shrilly. I could sense too much attention from the men, even though I was covered in a rather plain coat. I was happier when Stephen was back at the table.

"Here you go - one shandy. Cheers," he called and smiled, pushing his drink towards mine. "It's a bit of a dump here, really, isn't it? But it'll do to get out of the rain quickly."

We sipped.

"So, Sophia, Miss Best tells me that you're doing a good job in the office. Personally, I like the work you've been doing for us. Are you enjoying it?"

"Yes, actually I am," I said after a short pause. "I needed a job and Ronnie - you know Ronald in the High Street branch is my cousin, don't you? Well, he arranged it. I didn't think I would have much of an aptitude for it but it seems I might have."

"That's why I want to invite you out with me on a date," Stephen whispered and smirked. I blushed.

"I'm not sure I should be mixing business with pleasure, Stephen," I answered coyly.

"It's OK," he winked. "It's all business. I think I should have a word with Miss Best and see if she'll agree to have you come out with me on some appointments to view properties. You can take notes, write up the particulars and, if it goes OK, you can do more of them with some of the other fellas. What do you think? It'll give you an opportunity to learn more and, even though it's early days, I think you have real potential in this business - and I don't mean upstairs in the typing pool. You've got a flair for this, I think, and given half a chance you could shake us old farts up a bit. It's a pretty old-fashioned business but, personally, I think it's ready for some change."

"If Miss Best is OK with it, then I would love it."

"You're smart and have no preconceived ideas, so you must have an opinion on this. I'm sure you and Ronald talk about this too, don't you? You both share a flat, right? So you must talk about this stuff over the dinner table. He's a smart young chap and he's going places too. We should all join forces and turn this business upside down."

We chatted for another half hour and shared another shandy. Stephen opened up about the life he shared with his mother, who was living with the after-effects of a stroke that still left her struggling to cope after several years. Slowly, she seemed to be regaining her abilities and he was, unexpectedly, the devoted son who was giving up his independence to be there for her.

"My older brother is away at university and my father died a few years ago when both of us kids were still in school. I think that's what eventually led to mum's stroke. She was a fit, hard-working woman before that hit her. It's such a shame. It frustrates her so much. She and dad were both teachers. Now she has to stay at home all day and I do what I can to fill the void until she's back in control of her life, which I think she will be eventually. And what about your parents, Sophia? Do they live close by?" Stephen asked.

"They're both dead," What else could I say? I felt I had to prolong the lie, but Ronnie and I needed to talk about this and make sure we were consistent in our story.

"Oh! Sophia, I'm sorry to hear that. That must be so hard on you."

And so I told him the story as Ronnie would have told it. He commiserated and offered the usual platitudes, which I felt embarrassed to take, based as they were on a pack of lies.

"Well, drink up, and I'll escort you to your bus stop and keep you dry."

"Thanks for coming along with me, Sophia," he said as we made a dash for the bus, already idling at the stop. "We should do it again. And I'll talk to Miss Havisham about getting you out of the office."

"Miss Havisham?"

"You know, Miss Havisham - from 'Great Expectations'. That's what we call Miss Best. And, if you don't know, there's a story there too - hence the name," he said as he hoisted me onto the bus. "See you in the morning." He waved goodbye as he trotted off home.

When I got home Ronnie was pottering about in the kitchen. "You're late," he said. "I was just going to open a tin of beans but now you're back, maybe I'll run round to the chippy. We can share them over a can of lager. OK?"

"OK. It'll help maintain my fuller figure!" I smiled as he emerged from the kitchen, slipping his rain coat on.

"I'll be right back. You warm the oven."

In no time, he was back. The table was laid, the fish and chips re-heating in the oven. Ronnie split the can of lager and we sat down at the table.

"So, what made you late?"

"I was taken out for a drink by Stephen Cyrus. We popped into 'The Crown' for a couple of drinks and a chat. He's nicer than I thought. Comes across a bit too cocky, but I think that's a bit of a front. He's really quite sweet. His mother is handicapped by a stroke, did you know that? And he lives with her and helps her out."

"No, I didn't know, but it paints a nicer picture than I have of him."

"He thinks highly of you, so don't be too nasty." I said. "He thinks you're going places. Me too, as a matter of fact. Said I was well liked and making a good impression. He didn't make a pass at me or anything. It was all totally above board."

"Oh! Then he's going up more and more in my estimation. I thought he was the sort to try and roger you up against the bus shelter first chance he got."

"Ronnie! Don't be nasty! He's actually quite sweet. His parents were both teachers and his father died a long time ago. I think his mother is hoping to start teaching again but, in the meantime, he has his hands full. But he's always so cheerful. I have to give him that."

"Poor chap. I'll have to be more friendly to him."

"He asked about my parents, so I had to lie again. I told him they were dead. I don't like doing it but we've started it now," I said. "Do you think we're right?"

"Yes. Firstly, it makes people uncomfortable so they won't ask many questions and will quickly change the subject. And, second, it sounds a lot better if you say you come from a completely destroyed home rather than just a broken one. Otherwise people will wonder if some of the bad stuff has rubbed off on you and, besides, if you ever need to set the record straight, it's an easy lie to overlook or forgive. Just tell them you said it so that you didn't have to talk about all the bad stuff that went on at home. People will be very sympathetic."

"Yes, you're probably right." We sipped our lager and savoured our food.

"So, anything interesting in your day today?" I asked, not expecting anything much in response.

"Well, actually, it was quite an interesting afternoon. Or the last part anyway," Ronnie smiled slyly and gave me a sidelong glance.

"Hmm, something tells me I'm going to enjoy this. Something juicy?" I was very curious.

"You remember I told you that I had Toby Winters, the actor, for a client and that he had bought that big house along Parkside Drive? Well, he's just moved in and so I thought I would take a small housewarming gift over and say 'hi'. So, I did. I don't normally, but I was really curious about what the score was there."

"And did you …?" I asked, already anticipating the correct answer, otherwise he would have no story to tell. "Go on. I can tell you can barely contain yourself."

"Is it that obvious?" he cried, looking down at his crotch and smirking.

"Enough of that! You know what I mean …"

"OK. So, I turned up around four o'clock. I was pretty sure he was going to be around because he only moved in a few days ago and he told me he was going to be busy all week getting things organized before flying to Italy for some filming. Doesn't that sound glamorous? Flying to Italy for some filming. Do you think he'll see Sophia Loren or Gina Lollobrigida? He's had workmen there for weeks redecorating and putting in new bathrooms and kitchen. He's even putting a bed-sit over the garage for the housekeeper. Anyway, there was an Alfa Romeo and a Citroen in the drive. Very cosmopolitan, don't you think? So jet set!"

"I should lend him some of my 'Cosmopolitan' back issues! Or do you think he'd have them already…?"

"I think he'll have them already, based on today." Ronnie winked and continued. "With two cars outside, I didn't know if his friend would be there, or who would be there, but he was on his own and he gave me the complete tour. Sophe, you have to see it! It's a lovely old house and looks really elegant but, inside, it's been transformed. It's *so* modern, but in really good taste. He said he had a lot of input into the finishes so I think that's another indication that he has certain sensibilities, if you know what I mean. We boys are known for our good taste and, if that's any indication, he's got it in spades!"

"Is it all finished and furnished?" I asked.

"Yes, totally. I haven't seen any project like that go so fast before. Except for the flat over the garage it's all done and he showed me everything. He mentioned his friend and made it pretty clear that he wasn't living there. Funny. I got a pretty strong impression that he was going to be. Maybe there's been a bust-up there or something. There was no girlfriend mentioned, and certainly no wife."

"So, is it just him living in the house?" I asked. "That's an awful lot of house for just one person."

"Maybe I can help fill it." Ronnie whispered rather melodramatically. "Anyway, he had to go out so I didn't stay too long but, Sophia, I was definitely picking up all kinds of signals and then, when I was leaving, he put his arm around my shoulder and asked me to come to dinner this weekend! Can you believe it? Apparently, he's a whiz in the kitchen! If ever there was a sign for someone looking out for signs, that was it! Do you know any ordinary man who says he's a 'whiz in the kitchen'? I mean, really. I think he was trying to tell me something, don't you?"

I smiled.

"I'm not sure if it's just me or if there'll be other people there but I don't care. I'll find out when I get there. But what do you think of that? I'm so excited. I've never been to a film star's home before. Not that he's exactly a film star, but you know what I mean. His star is definitely in the ascendency. Don't tell anyone. This is between you and me. I'm not going to say anything in case it compromises him or anyone or anything afterwards. OK?"

"Of course. I won't say anything, but only on one condition," I said harshly.

"What's that?"

"That you tell me *every*thing that happens that night," I cried, jumping up and down in my seat. "This is just far too good to miss."

"I think this deserves another lager, don't you, Sophe? I'll go get one from the kitchen."

"Lager today but champagne next week." I giggled and raised my glass, totally oblivious to the crack in the pavement that I was about to trip over.

22

A Night to Remember

Ronnie's story...

DINNER WITH TOBY WAS SET FOR Saturday evening. I was working that morning but had all afternoon to get ready. Sophia was going to join me that afternoon to shop for something special to wear. We talked about it all week. God knows it seemed like the most exciting event of my life, so what else were we going to do? It seemed destined to be the most exciting night of her life as well and she wasn't even going to be there.

We were going to enjoy it to the limit. We decided that I would wear my best black dress pants; but should I wear a jacket and a tie? Or should I wear a polo neck and a jacket or just a polo neck? Or should I wear a shirt and cravat? Styles were changing by the day, even for men, and I didn't know whether to be a little behind the times, on time or ahead. For a queer this sort of decision was exhausting, believe me.

In the end, and with much input from Sophia, I decided to wear my almost-new tweedy jacket, more blacks, blues and reds than a typical tweed and, with that, I would wear a new polo neck sweater in some matching bold colour. At least that narrowed down the purchases to one thing. With it, I would wear my newest black shoes, a pair of Chelsea boots - black of course - that I cherished passionately.

On Saturday afternoon, after the office closed for the day at noon, Sophia and I went up to London to find me the perfect sweater. We scoured Oxford Street, hit the King's Road and amused ourselves on Carnaby Street, but it was in a small shop off the King's Road that we found it. A rich shade of burgundy red cashmere that set off all the colours in the jacket without being garish. It was perfect and we celebrated with coffee at a little Italian café on the corner.

We got a table at the window and stared out at the world rushing by. As we sipped our cappuccinos we admired it all. Mini-skirts were everywhere, even in winter, accompanied by thigh high boots and geometric styles in all colours. Flowing tresses or pixie cuts, it didn't matter. The main thing was to look different and feel fabulous. Or was it the other way around? Or did it even matter? But how was it possible that all those people, trying so hard to be different, just ended up looking so much the same?

I gazed discreetly at Sophia and considered how much her life really had changed, in large measure thanks to me. I was proud of my creation. As she sat there, demurely, I marvelled again at the transformation, as I had done so many times before.

I simply could never tire of it.

Hers really was a Cinderella story.

Corny but true.

Fortuitously, she turned out to have all the right attributes to become a real, natural beauty. Who would have thought that, tucked under too much skin and bad hair, along with the benefit of some teenage hormones, were the makings of a lovely, bright, intelligent and sexy young woman. I couldn't deny it. I had become her Prince Charming.

What a great team we had become!

As we made our way home on the tube, I was full of anticipation for the evening. I had no idea whether it was to be just the two of us, which I somehow doubted, or whether it would be a group and, if so, how big and who would be there. I had never mixed with the famous before. Not even the vaguely or barely famous and certainly nobody with a name that half the people in Britain would recognise. This was most certainly a first and I was thrilled. Well, I mean, what twenty-six-year-old hot-blooded male wouldn't be?

When we were home, I took a long bath and a long time getting myself ready. By half-past six I had primped and preened enough that even I was satisfied.

"You look fabulous!" Sophia exclaimed.

"Do I? Even for the rich and famous? This is my one chance to make a big first impression."

"Oh, you'll do that alright! Everybody'll want you tonight. Even the girls!"

"Well that could prove interesting. Maybe I'll have me one of those threesomes." I cried. "OK. Wish me luck. I'm going now. I think I'll walk. It's a dry evening and it's not that far away."

And picking up my bottle of Italian red, suitably wrapped, I left. The evening was clear and fresh and I strolled along the High Street, past closed shops, busy town pubs and jumbled rows of comfortable middle-class Victorian houses that gave way to more affluent, upper-class villas the closer I got to the Common and Parkside Drive.

The homes here were still traditional Victorian but much larger and in more spacious, beautifully tended gardens than the homes that I had passed. This was where the money was, that was clear. Lights glowed in many rooms, showing off interesting interiors with fine paintings, rich colours and dramatic lighting. Some were still old and dull but they were increasingly few and far between, as I had noticed in my few years of dealing with homes here.

And then I was at Toby's house, all aglow.

And, seemingly, full of people.

The house was a splendid, spacious, freshly painted, double-fronted Victorian with wings, so the garden was wide enough to allow for a semi-circular drive that, that evening, was full of cars. I rang the doorbell and after a few seconds, Toby answered, all smiles and full of good cheer.

Toby was handsome - remarkably handsome, truth be told - in the typical way the British seemed to love their actors. Not too tall, he was slim and wiry with an oval face and refined features; just a hint of a dimple in the chin. Not at all like the over-sized, ruggedly handsome hunks that the Americans seemed to produce. These British editions were of a gentler, almost effete, appearance that displayed charm and sensitivity. These were the sort of men that women wanted to mother and snuggle, not be ravaged by. But maybe both if they were honest with themselves.

He had a head of thick, long, fine, sandy-blond hair, hanging just over his collar and flopping over his forehead in a very casual, boyish style which was enhanced by piercing greenish-blue eyes that made his whole face light up, just as it did now, as he invited me in. I could tell by his casual dress - tight-fitting jeans, a collarless, cream cambric shirt tucked into them, and wide, woven brown leather belt with large brass buckle and brown cowboy boots - that I was going to be over-dressed.

But that was fine because I knew I looked great and felt greater. He had his shirt unbuttoned to the centre of his chest, exposing a v-shaped expanse of fuzzy chest hair with a small silver pendant hanging around his neck. It was a look that could have worked badly but, on Toby, it was vaguely bohemian, working magically to further enhance his appeal. The animal magnetism that worked so well for him on the screen was all too clear to see in real life.

He beamed. "Come in! Come in! Join the party. Most people are here but they've only just arrived." I followed him into the large front drawing room where the guests were mingling. There were about twenty people there, most of whom I didn't recognise but there were a few that I did. My knees weakened as I recognised Dirk Bogarde and Dusty Springfield, two of my favourite famous people. I tried to hide my amazement as much as possible as Toby introduced me to the group.

"I'd like to introduce Ronald. Ronald is the person who found me this fabulous house. He's the local estate agent and if anyone else wants to move close by, he's the man to call. Right, Ronald?"

"I suppose I am," I said, rather flustered and red-faced. I was welcomed into the party and introduced to most of the guests who, it turned out, were a mix of old friends and business connections, including a couple of film directors, a BBC executive and a lawyer or two, along with spouses. For me, Dirk and Dusty were the stars of the show and, just on their own, were worth the evening. As well as Toby Winters, of course. Needless to say, I barely spoke to either of them, I was so intimidated and tongue-tied, drinking a little too much in order to loosen my tongue and lower my anxiety level.

Everyone was so relaxed and comfortable with one another, regardless of who was with whom and why. Dusty was there with a beautiful, tall black woman in a figure-hugging dress that showed every fabulous curve. It was all very broad-minded and modern and I was loving every moment of it.

Toby turned out to be a whizz at organizing the kitchen. The housekeeper, Maria, was a stunning blond with a very Scandinavian look; not at all housekeeping material. More like heart stopping and house stealing material. She was charming and discreet as she made sure everything worked perfectly and that everyone was provided for. She and Toby worked seamlessly together, almost as equals, and I wondered what that relationship was really all about.

As the evening wore on and the alcohol kicked in, I settled comfortably into the atmosphere and spent a lot of time talking to a cinematographer and his wife. As the party drew to a close, we were amongst the few remaining and I was fascinated by his stories of life on the sets - the tantrums, the dramas, the tears. I thought of Norma.

It was almost 1:30.

"Time I should be heading home. I've had a wonderful evening. I can't believe I met Dusty Springfield and Dirk Bogarde both in one evening. I can't wait to tell Sophia. She will die with envy."

"Then we should do it again," said Toby before emptying his glass as well. "And you can invite her."

"Well, thank you. I'll look forward to that very much, but I had better go now and let you get some rest."

"Would you like me to call a taxi?" Maria asked.

"No. Thank you. I'll walk from here and it'll give me a chance to clear my head. It's still dry outside so I'll enjoy the fresh air."

"OK. You know where we are and you have my number," said Toby putting his arm around me and leading me to the front door. "You looked great tonight, by the way, in case I didn't tell you already."

"Oh, thanks! Sophia will be pleased to hear that since she chose the sweater today and virtually put my wardrobe together for tonight."

"A woman of taste. I like that. That's a good omen. You must definitely bring her over some time soon."

"Oh, and don't forget, you have my number too," I said "If you ever want to use it."

We said our good nights before I stepped out into the night air. I strolled down the drive and turned around once for a final wave. Toby was still in the porch under the elegant hanging lamp and waved back. I carried on down the road and thought how much Sophia was going to enjoy this whole story.

The walk home helped to clear my head and I tried not to stumble up the stairs to the flat. As quietly as I could, I undid the lock and entered the flat. "Shit!" I spat through gritted teeth as I made my way through the unlit sitting room only to stumble into an end table, tipping a vase that shattered on the floor. "Shit! Shit! Shit!" I spat again and again.

"Ronnie, is that you?" Sophia, slurring with sleep, called weakly from her bedroom.

"I'm so sorry, Sophe. I was trying to be quiet and not wake you."

"Rubbish! You have to come here right now and tell me how it went. Please! Please! Please!" She was clearly waking up, and quickly.

"OK. Let me get a glass of water and I'll be right there. I'll get you one as well."

I poured two glasses and carried them over. Sophia was pushing herself up and resting on her girly pink pillows in the dim light from the sitting room.

"Let me put a light on," I said as I leaned over and switched on her bedside lamp. I grabbed both her wrists and pushed my face in close to hers. "If I never have an evening that good again, I'll be happy. It was wonderful!"

"Well, tell me. Tell me."

"Toby was great and made sure I felt comfortable with everybody. There were directors there, cinematographers, a couple of lawyers and, you'll never guess, Dusty Springfield and Dirk Bogarde."

She squealed.

"Can you believe that? Two of my favourite celebrities in the whole wide world were together in the same room. I could hardly speak, but Toby loosened me up with a few drinks. It was brilliant. And, guess what? He's on my team. I'm sure of it."

"Oh my god!" Sophia cried and we both squealed with laughter.

"Honest to god, Sophe, if I die tonight I'll die a happy man and you can put that on my gravestone! Toby is definitely one of the boys. He said as much without actually saying the words. He put his arm around my shoulders and hugged me when I was leaving and said that I have to come back and - listen to this - *I have to bring you*! Yes, you have to come as well."

Sophia's eyes widened. "You wouldn't joke about a thing like that, would you?" she whispered warily as she pushed herself higher up on her pillows.

"Would I be that cruel? I told them your whole life story and he was really intrigued. Not all of them. I just told him and his cousin after the others had gone. Apparently, she lives there with him as his housekeeper. She seems really nice too. But what a coincidence, eh? Here I am living with my female younger cousin and there he is, living with his female younger cousin."

"I suppose he's a better cook than her too?" Sophia added wryly.

"Of course. The food was delicious and the company was fun. I couldn't have asked for a better evening, Sophe, I really couldn't. That investment in the sweater was well worth it, even if I was over-dressed. I'm going to have lots of dreamy nights over this experience, I can tell you. And talking of sleep, it's time I got some. Night - night."

I gave Sophia a kiss on the forehead. "That's plenty for both of us to sleep on tonight, I reckon, don't you? See you in the morning."

Despite all the wine, I couldn't sleep, at least not for long. As soon as Sophia started stirring in the morning I got up and made us both some good, strong coffee and we stretched out in the living room, as I slowly shook the torpor from my head.

"So, what are you going to do for an encore?" asked Sophia with a smirk.

I laughed.

"I don't think I'll ever top that, do you? Unless I get myself stuck in that circle which, actually, wouldn't be difficult if I worked at it. I think Toby really took a shine to me and I really liked him, but I don't want to push too hard. I'll have to wait and see if he makes the next move. I don't want to be the first to do it. I'm not going to just let it drift off though."

"Do you think he was serious about meeting me?" Sophia asked.

"I'm sure of it. Anyway, I'll make sure it happens. If he doesn't call me in the next week, I'll call him and charm him into getting together. You know me, Sophe. Prince Charming personified. Nobody can resist me until they get to know me. Isn't that right?" I laughed.

"You are totally irresistible any time, Ronnie, and you know it."

"Should we call Ellen and Peter and suggest the pub for lunch? I want to tell them all about my night and, besides, I think I might need a bit of the hair of the dog. And, right now, I need a nice juicy bacon and egg sandwich to soak up all that alcohol."

I slipped into the kitchen.

"Would you like one?"

23

Falling! Falling!

Sophia's story...

BUT THE NEXT DAY IT WAS back to reality.

Stephen arranged for me to accompany him that week on the first of our joint property inspections so that I could see first-hand what an estate agent's life was like on the front line. We did two that week and Stephen always managed to arrange for them to be at the end of the workday, so we could enjoy a drink together before making our separate ways home.

I had to admit that I was finding him more and more attractive. He was bright and amusing and he had a wicked sense of humour. He was also good to look at and that certainly helped. On our second outing, he asked me out on a date.

"Sophia, I'm sure you've noticed how attractive you are. And I'm sure you've noticed that I've noticed that," he said bluntly, arms resting on the table in the lounge bar and looking straight at me.

"Yes, I suppose I have." I couldn't deny the blindingly obvious.

"And I think you like me, don't you?" he asked.

"Yes. You're very nice."

"Well, I suppose I can live with 'nice' for now, until I can get a more exciting adjective out of you. Would you like to come out with me? Maybe we can go to the pictures. We could go and see 'The Graduate'. Have you seen it? It's supposed to be really good. It's playing at the Odeon, Leicester Square. We could go for a drink afterwards."

"When did you think to go? This Saturday?" I asked.

"You name it. I'll make it work."

And so we made a plan. We would meet at Wimbledon Station at six o'clock on Saturday evening and take the train up to the city. I told Ronnie that evening, over dinner, but he didn't seem too pleased.

"Be careful, Sophe. I'm not sure about that man. I know you say he's nicer than he seemed but that could just be a bit of deceit on his part. Don't forget your goals. You don't want him getting in the way and spoiling everything. He can't offer you anything more than a million other men can and that's not what you want."

"It's only a date, Ronnie! You don't need to be so protective. I'm not planning on falling for the first man who looks at me twice."

Ronnie laughed. "Sophia, if you were going to fall for the first man to look at you twice, it would have happened years ago. In case you hadn't noticed, half the men who pass you do a double take and the other half just didn't see you or they would have to. You're a knockout, Sophe, so don't waste it."

"I'm not going to. I still want to stick to my plan and Stephen isn't part of that."

But, of course, it wasn't quite that simple. Is it ever? Our date went well and we had fun. Stephen treated me like a princess and didn't put a foot wrong, or even a hand. He was charming.

He invited me out again and we had a lovely time. We did it again, and then we did it again. By the fifth time I was feeling very warm and comfortable with him. Ronnie, on the other hand, was not so charmed.

"So, are you seeing your friend, Stephen, again this weekend, Sophia?" He asked as we sat in the sitting room watching television one evening after supper.

"He hasn't asked me yet, but he probably will." I avoided his gaze.

"What would that be? Your sixth date? Don't forget what I said. Men are mostly out for one thing and you don't have the experience yet to tell the jerks from the nice guys. Don't give him what he wants."

"And what does he want?"

"The same thing that all men want. To get his leg over. But he's got a lot more hard work to do before he earns that prize. You know that, right? The last thing I want to see is him spoil your chances. This is all making me very nervous. I don't want him fucking up all our hard work."

I rarely heard Ronnie get rattled or lose his temper.

"It's OK." I said. "I'm just pleased to have a man to go around with and feel desired. I'm sure it'll happen lots of times again but, right now, I'm just enjoying it. And besides, I know him and I know a lot about him so I feel safe. It's not as though I'm going out with a complete stranger."

"Oh, and I'm not a man, am I?"

"You know what I mean - a man who might make a pass at me."

"I'm not sure if that's a good or bad thing. It would be easy to let your guard down with this bloke and then it's too late," he said sharply, staring across at me. "I'm sorry, Sophia. I'm not trying to be hard on you. I just know what these chaps want to get up to and the only person that gets hurt is almost always the girl. I have your best interests at heart. You know that, don't you?"

I got up and went over to Ronnie and, from behind his chair, put my arms around his neck and, with a sideways movement, leant over and put a kiss on his cheek and squeezed. "You know I love you. You're the best person in the world for a girl like me. I wouldn't do anything to hurt you. You know that too, right?"

Then I really messed up.

And I had been doing so well.

There was a glimmer of awareness that someone was following me. Stalking they would call it today. Not that we had such a word for it then. It didn't really have a name, or an identity for that matter. All I knew was that someone was lurking about, watching me. It was a strange feeling which, at first, I couldn't put my finger on until I caught sight of him one evening as I was leaving work.

I was standing on the front steps, looking across the street and there he was - my father. I hadn't seen him since I had left home all those months and years ago and now he had frozen me to the spot; I knew I couldn't stay like that. If he saw me watching him before I had had time to arrange my thoughts, then I would be lost.

I quickly turned on my heels and dashed back into the office, nearly knocking over Miss Best in the process. I was visibly disconcerted but managed to camouflage the worst of it.

"Oops! Sorry - I forgot something."

"It must be important judging by the rush."

"It is a bit, yes." I smiled as broadly as I could while I trembled inwardly. "Someone's birthday card. They'll be disappointed if I don't get it in the post." I dashed back upstairs to the typing pool, now unlit, where I could overlook the street unnoticed.

He was still there, dressed in an old donkey jacket and looking seedy. He was falling apart at the seams and I was able to take my time in the shadows to observe him in all his fading glory. The teddy-boy good looks that had charmed their way into too many girls' and women's hearts - and knickers too for that matter - were sadly fading. There before me was a rather pathetic looking, middle-aged man, huddling inside his coat, and struggling to hold onto the years. His face was blotchy, his still-Brylcreemed, slicked back hair was going grey and he was getting a paunch.

I bet he didn't pull many girls anymore.

Dragged was more like it.

Kicking and screaming.

This was the man who had turned my heart to stone, ruined my childhood, broke my trust and become the devil in our house. The man I was recovering from. And here he was, his very presence dragging me back to the bottom of the hill that I had been struggling to climb.

His attention was shifting but it always came back to the front door of the office. He knew that I would be here. How long had he known and how often had he done this? I had had a sense of someone but no idea of the times that I might have been completely oblivious to his presence. I suppose it was some consolation that nothing had ever happened, at least not yet. He hadn't approached me or, worse, attacked me.

I decided to leave by the back door to the lane and onto the side street. There I could catch a bus unobserved and buy myself some time to gather my thoughts and make a plan.

But I couldn't hide for long. I couldn't use the back door forever before he figured out that something had changed and then he would change his tactics. Clearly he had a purpose and every evening now I checked to see if he was there before I left for home. I hadn't told Ronnie, or anyone else for that matter. I needed time to think and to decide how to react. Did I have the courage to face him alone, or would I need some help?

It was another week before I saw him again and he was just leaning quietly in the doorway behind the bus stop, looking frequently towards my office door and, again, I slipped out the back.

Next week, same thing, same day, but this time he got distracted by a woman. Of course. A cheap tart with peroxide hair and far too much makeup. I would have taken her for a prostitute except I knew he would never pay for what they sold. He'd take it though, if it was on offer and, tonight, it looked like it might be because he was thoroughly distracted and barely glanced my way.

She was game alright and aging as badly and sadly as he was. But beggars couldn't be choosers and she seemed to be begging for it alright. I was sure he was going to choose her over me. They talked for a few minutes before she shook her head to the left, towards the pub. That's where he followed her, so I was able to make my escape once again.

This continued for weeks and weeks, either on a Monday or Tuesday, and I could only assume that he was working in the area and clearly knew more about me than I cared for him to know.

Did he know where I lived?

Had he followed me home?

Listened at my front door?

The thought gave me the creeps. How much didn't I know about his sneaky habits and would I suffer at the end of it? I didn't know what to do. I didn't want to talk about this to anyone in the family. Opening up closets and tossing out the ghosts that I had worked so hard to stash away, out of sight, held no appeal for me.

If anyone should know, it was Ronnie. He would know how to react. But this was irrational, emotional, frightening stuff and, while Ronnie could be counted on to react calmly and sensibly, I didn't know if I could, once my determination had been breached.

There was one person who might be able to help, I thought. Stephen Cyrus. We had grown quite friendly and talked freely, yet he was completely independent of the situation. A curious by-stander. An on-looker who could check out the damage, point at the bad guy and say "Yep. He did it. Now what are you going to do about it." Which he did - to a point - until he caused as much damage himself.

We had been to the pictures. We saw 'Georgy Girl'. All the famous names of the sixties were in it – Lynn Regrave, James Mason, Alan Bates, Charlotte Rampling and there, on the screen, were shadows of my future life. Or my future life as I foresaw it then. A young girl marrying a rich husband for lots of reasons but love.

After the movie, Stephen and I stopped for coffee and talked about what we had seen. Even though he had enjoyed it, poor Stephen thoroughly disapproved of the inappropriate behaviour. Nobody seemed aware of how odd, shallow, egocentric - even a little horrible - the sixties were while they were happening; we were all so wrapped up in it. But Stephen clearly got a whiff of something rotten.

"That film just showed everything that's going wrong these days." Stephen sniffed prissily as he picked up his cup. "Don't get me wrong, it was a good film but what a load of wankers!"

"Why? I thought it was very modern."

"That's what I'm saying. That's the problem. Rich man wants to take a mistress. Girl says no and shacks up with girlfriend's husband after girlfriend leaves, then boyfriend leaves and girl ends up marrying rich man. I mean, blimey, what sort of behaviour is that?"

"It's only a film."

"Yes, but a film about real life, supposedly, and the girlfriend's had two abortions, without even telling the bloke - who's the father by the way, and should be consulted, don't you think?"

Oh, don't be such an old fuddy-duddy." I laughed. "Don't tell me you want to stick to the so-called good old days? Till death us do part and all that."

"Nothing wrong with that. It worked for my mum and dad and I bet it worked for yours as well." He looked quite smug.

So I let him have it.

With both barrels.

So, now, someone else besides me knew what was hanging in the back of my closet. He hadn't been given full visitation rights but, for better or for worse, he now knew far more than anyone else.

"Blimey, Sophia. That's a right old mess, isn't it? I can see why you left home so soon and how Ronnie fits into the picture now. He's like a brother to you."

"Better than a brother. I've got a brother so I know how they can be and mine's a proper sod. Ronnie's like the best father, brother and uncle all rolled into one, so don't be saying a word against him." My voice was rising.

"OK. Calm down. Have I ever said anything nasty about him? He's a good bloke. Not sure he's my type but he's a good bloke."

"And what's that supposed to mean?" I sniffed.

"Just that he's not the kind of bloke I'd hang around with, but that's not a criticism. He's just different from me. He's got a few airs and graces, that's all."

"There's nothing wrong with having a bit of class." I was getting quite snippy by now. I sensed that he was zeroing in on Ronnie's secret life and I had to squash any thought of that, for Ronnie's sake.

"I'm just saying, that's all. He'd probably say the same thing about me, only in reverse. A bit uncouth and vulgar for him. A bit of a wide boy is what he'd say about me."

"And you're not?"

"Yeah, I am actually. But I'm nice with it." He winked and grinned. "And don't say you hadn't noticed or you wouldn't be hanging around with me, right?"

"I suppose. But don't think you're so special, mister. There's plenty more like you in the sea and I plan to hook me a big one."

"No chance for me then?"

"Not unless they make you a partner. And soon."

"Then I suppose I'd better seduce you as quick as I can and be on my way."

"Fat chance!"

"So, anyway, getting back to the subject at hand. What are you going to do about your dad? Are you going to confront him?

"I don't know. He just makes me cold all over. I don't think I can stand up to him."

"Why don't you tell Ronnie and maybe the two of you can try and talk some sense into him."

"He doesn't listen to sense. He likes to cause trouble. That's what he enjoys the most. That and drinking and womanizing."

"He sounds lovely."

"Oh, he's a star alright. It gives me the creeps just thinking about him again. Just when I had almost forgotten."

"So, what did he do to you?"

"Enough. And that's all I'm going to say."

"Do you want me to have a go at him? You point him out from the office and I'll go over and have a word. That way nobody needs to know except me. Not Ronnie. Nobody. Just us."

It was very tempting.

"Let me think about it."

So I did and a plan was hatched which was executed the following week.

"I have to tell the truth about something," I said before the meeting. "When you go over to talk to him, you'll have to say that Edith sent you."

"Edith? Why Edith?"

"Because that's my name. My real name. Sophia is the name I chose as part of my new life."

"So how many other secrets have you got stashed away?"

"A few. But you know most of them now and, who knows, you might get to know the rest if you're very, very good."

"Let's see if I get through this alive and then we can talk about the rest."

"You will. He's not violent outside the house."

The implication wasn't lost on Stephen.

"I have a few secrets too, while we're playing the truth game."

"Oh?"

"Yes. Well, my mother's as healthy as the Queen and my father is still busy managing a furniture factory." He looked at me sheepishly and shrugged. "I thought you'd take pity on me if you heard a hard luck story. Sorry. Like you, I don't make a habit of lying but, of course, you don't know that, do you? It could all be a pack of lies, couldn't it?"

"I suppose we both have a bit of confidence to earn back. Besides, if you do this for me, I'll overlook it until it ever happens again. Then - watch out."

He beamed. "It won't. You have my word on it. Not that that means anything right now, but it will."

The following Tuesday, Stephen came upstairs at closing time and we chatted as I kept an eye out of the window and, sure enough, he was there.

Same donkey jacket. Puffing on the same old Woodbines. Same smug 'fancy me do yer, darlin'?' look in his eye. Cocky enough to make me want to kick his head in and I would have loved for Stephen to do it, but I knew that was asking far too much.

"Action stations," I whispered sharply.

"Where?"

"Guess."

"Oh, that's easy," he laughed after a few seconds of scouring the pavement for likely candidates. "Him on the bank steps, yeah? Smoking the cigarette and staring at all the tarts." He was right. "Stay here. I'll be right back."

He was. The conversation was short, with few gestures and little animation. In a matter of minutes, Stephen was back.

"Well?"

"He's the one."

I rolled my eyes. "I bloody well know that, Stephen. But what did he say?"

"He asked if I was your boyfriend."

"And."

"I said yes."

"You cheeky bugger. You are not."

"I know that – but I might be, right? After what I'm doing for you. And, besides, one good turn deserves another." He winked the wink that boys give when they're after only one thing. "Besides, I thought he would pay a lot more attention to me if he thought I was your boyfriend. And he did. I could tell." He paused to light a cigarette and squinted as the smoke caught his eye. "He wants to meet you. He'll be here this time next week and he's OK with me being there to play chaperone. You just try and keep me away and if you do, I'll be a fly on the wall instead. That meeting I most definitely want to see."

"It's not funny."

"Sorry. I know that. I find the whole thing intriguing, is all I meant." He puffed on his cigarette. "We can go to a pub and have 'a chat', is what he said. A nice little chat."

"I can assure you there'll be nothing nice about it."

And there wasn't.

Nothing nice at all.

To enjoy your ***FREE*** copy of the fun-filled novella '***Fun Is On Its Way***', a prequel to '***The Cost of Loving***' series, and to join the growing list of Sophia's followers, be sure to follow this link below.

http://www.martinhumphriesauthor.com/free-novella

About Volume Two

Sophia is ruthlessly determined to achieve the sort of success that she hadn't, until now, dared to dream of. Thanks to Ronnie, life seems ready to take a dramatic and unexpected turn that could complete the job that he alone started, and where love will not be required. But does Sophia's coming of age reach the triumphant climax that just might be waiting for her? It's a roller-coaster ride full of glorious highs and frightening lows, especially when history catches up with her to destroy the greatest day of her young life. Will she survive it? And, if she does, how will she deal with it? And will she seek revenge?.

About the Author

Martin Humphries is a first time author who, once he started writing, couldn't stop. Now, after five industrious years, Martin has completed ***The Cost of Loving*** series of which ***Can't Buy Me Love (1964 - 1967)*** and ***Love for Sale (1967 – 1970)*** comprise the first two volumes.

The four volumes of ***Free Love, Love Don't Cost a Thing, The Price of Love*** and ***Love Hurts*** complete this dramatic coming of age story that spreads over two decades and two continents. It is a bittersweet, rollercoaster ride of a life lived in the spotlight and with the dark side well hidden from view.

After so many decades of life, Martin is full of stories that need to be told and is busy working on several of them right now, including a sequel series to ***The Cost of Loving*** series that follows Sophia through ***The Plague Years*** of the 1980's and beyond.

Martin lives quietly on Gabriola Island, one of the Gulf Islands in the archipelago stretching north from the American border between Vancouver and Vancouver Island, on Canada's wild and rugged west coast.

It's a wonderful place to write, surrounded by so many other creative people, his partner of twenty three years, Paul, and the best dog in the world, Alfie.

Martin's web site is www.martinhumphriesauthor.com or he can also be found on Facebook.

By Martin Humphries

The Cost of Loving Series
Can't Buy Me Love (1964 - 1967)
Love for Sale (1967 - 1970)
Free Love (1970 - 1973)
Love Don't Cost a Thing (1973 - 1975)
The Price of Love (1975 - 1976)
Love Hurts (1976 - 1984)

Fun Is On Its Way
A prequel to *The Cost of Loving* series

Coming Soon:

Life After Death -Volume one of *The Plague Years Series* which follows Sophia's life where *The Cost of Loving* ends.
Points of No Return

For information on the next episodes of Sophia's life, follow the link below to get the latest updates.
http://www.martinhumphriesauthor.com/costofloving

Acknowledgments

I would like to offer my heartfelt appreciation to all my friends and colleagues who have encouraged me to move forward to complete the daunting task of writing some 400,000 words of fiction when I had never written more than a few pages in my life before. I also want to thank them for their opinion and feedback that has allowed me to hone the six volumes into something that I am truly proud of.

I especially want to thank my partner Paul Ryan, and my dog Alfie, who gave me the freedom to spend so many hours hunched over my computer, and for the vital comments that made all three volumes even better.

Specifically, I would like to thank Edie Hildreth and Janet Hodgson who, as my very first readers, were willing to immerse themselves in initial drafts and offer their thoughts and observations on how the story could be improved. Also, thanks to the editors at Writer's Services who pointed me in the right direction whenever I veered off course.

I should also thank Helen Gurley Brown whose death was the seed from which the whole story germinated. Thanks also go to my client - who shall be nameless - whose bankruptcy left me with hundreds of thousands of dollars in unpaid fees which I resolved would be the lemons from which lemonade would be made. This story, and other books in progress, are that lemonade.

I hope you enjoyed reading ***Can't Buy Me Love*** and will continue to enjoy the story with the other five books in the series. There is no greater honour for writers than to know that their works are enjoyed by their readers. If you enjoyed this book and any others in the series, please tell others and consider posting a reader review online, for there is no greater support you can give than your word-of mouth recommendation.

Can't Buy Me Love (1964-1967)

Written and published by Martin Humphries

Cover by Bryan McCrae
Book design and layout by Human Powered Design

ISBN: 978-0-9959444-3-5

Printed in Great Britain
by Amazon

72074091R00144